THE FATHER

BOOK 3 IN THE GALBRAITH SERIES

JOHN NICHOLL

First published in Great Britain in 2022 by Boldwood Books Ltd.

Cover Design by Head Design

Cover Photography: Shutterstock

A CIP catalogue record for this book is available from the British Library.

Paperback ISBN 978-1-80426-359-4

Large Print ISBN 978-1-80426-358-7

Hardback ISBN 978-1-80426-360-0

Ebook ISBN 978-1-80426-356-3

Kindle ISBN 978-1-80426-357-0

Audio CD ISBN 978-1-80426-365-5

MP3 CD ISBN 978-1-80426-364-8

Digital audio download ISBN 978-1-80426-363-1

Boldwood Books Ltd
23 Bowerdean Street
London SW6 3TN
www.boldwoodbooks.com

A NOTE TO THE READER

While fictional, this book was inspired by true events. It draws on the author's experiences as a police officer and child protection social worker. The story contains content that some readers may find upsetting. It is dedicated to survivors everywhere.

1

We have the capacity for such creative beauty but also such unspeakable horror. I suspect I know that at least as well as most. It's a sad reality I can't deny, however much I'd like to eradicate certain aspects of my past.

I'm an adult now, Mr Anthony Mailer, or Tony, as I'm known to friends and family. A thirty-seven-year-old husband and father of one, a reasonably successful journalist living in rural west Wales, close to an estuary beach, a fifteen-minute drive from town. But I was a child when my story began. A seven-year-old boy growing up in an ordinary family in a beautiful land. But danger lurked in the most unexpected places.

I encountered a monster, a predator who hid not in darkness, but in plain sight. Appearances can be so very deceptive. If only such men came with a warning branded on their foreheads: *danger, beware, don't come near, stay away!*

Even uttering my tormentor's name is something of a challenge. Dr David Galbraith still dominates my life in many ways, even though I haven't seen him since childhood. Does that sound ridiculous to you? Can you make any sense of this statement?

Well, yes or no, as crazy as it may seem to some, it's true. Galbraith's name may mean nothing to you, but it means so very much to me. He was my doctor, a *supposed* therapist – a consultant child psychiatrist, no less – and a deviant who targeted, groomed and assaulted his young patients at will. He helped some, keeping up the façade of apparent respectability, but offended against others, preadolescent boys who fitted his victim profile, as I did. He hid his true nature from the world because it suited him to do so. And he hid it well. He was liked, respected, seen as a pillar of the community, someone to look up to, revered. But I knew him as only a survivor can know him. There is nothing good to say about that man. I feel anger, I feel hate, and sadness too. Galbraith was a creature devoid of sympathy or goodness; a sadistic, psychopathic criminal of the worst possible kind. I want readers to know that right from the very start. It's the foundation of my story, the basis of all that comes next.

Galbraith still haunts me after all this time. I guess time doesn't heal all wounds. It may do for some, but it certainly hasn't for me. He visits me often in my weaker moments, when my mind wanders back in time, or I lie awake at night, falling in and out of fitful sleep until dawn's welcome light drives away the sound and sight of him. But he always comes back. He's there somewhere in the near distance, even in my happier times, when I'm relaxing with friends and family, watching television, listening to music, reading a favourite book, or sitting in the sun.

I'm an adult now, but I mourn for the boy I knew. I feel sad about his lost childhood. I have a loving, intelligent, beautiful wife, a healthy, full-of-life daughter of my own, a comfortable home, and a well-paying job, all the trappings of a seemingly successful life. Anyone looking in may think I have it made, that I'm living the dream. But first impressions can be notoriously deceptive. Even all of those bright, shiny things aren't sufficient to send the past to oblivion. The symptoms of post-traumatic stress are still a feature of my life, the flashbacks too regular, the nightmares too real, my overprotective tendencies often at the forefront of my mind. I experience wild mood swings, sometimes when I least expect them. The black dog of depression visits all too often. I worry about my daughter's safety to such an extent that it sometimes negatively affects her life. And I drink too much, one skull-splitting hangover after another. A day rarely passes without a drink or two to numb my troubled mind. And so, things need to change. If they don't, Galbraith will have won. And that's something I can't let happen. He's taunted me for long enough. It's time to make it stop.

* * *

Writing this book is my attempt to make sense of my past, to understand the events that have shaped my life, and, to some extent, made me the man I am.

Writing is an exorcism of sorts, a prolonged therapeutic exercise that I hope will prove healing. I plan to tell my story with brutal honesty. If I'm going to do this, if it's going to mean something, I have to bare my soul. And everything I'm going to tell you is accurate. I know, I lived it, I was there. I accept the telling won't be easy, but nightmares thrive in darkness. I've tried hiding from the events of those dark days for thirty long years. I've tried pushing the memories from my mind time and again without success. There's no room for denial. I have to face what happened, up close and personal.

And so, I'll tell my story, I'll shine a light on the worst times of my life. And in doing so, I hope to feel better. I hope I find the solace I so desperately crave, both for my sake and that of my wife and child. I'm not an easy person to live with; that's the truth of it.

There's only so much people can put up with, however much they love you.

But this isn't just my story. I've worked hard in preparation for the telling. I've undertaken extensive research before reaching this point. It's something I'm good at, a skill I've honed over years in my professional role for one newspaper or another. My story won't all be based on faded childhood memories. Others were involved, many were affected. It's their story too. I've read and watched the various news reports relevant to the case. I've interviewed the key professionals, or at least those who agreed to talk. I've spoken with Galbraith's ex-wife. I've even spoken to a convicted sex offender who knew the *real* Galbraith. And I've discussed events with my family – my mother, Molly, my father, Mike, and my big sister, Siân. All three thought this endeavour unwise at first, and to a degree, they still do. But they've come to realise my writing is something that can't be avoided. Whether they'll read the book if published, I can't say. That has to be their decision, and not mine. Only they can decide. And that applies to you too. The book will contain content that some readers may find disturbing. There's no avoiding that reality. What happened, happened. It's the nature of the subject matter. So, please bear that in mind as you turn the pages.

* * *

The available media reports gave me the basics of the story in addition to my memories, but the interviews provided the detail. Revelations that were at times both shocking and traumatic. Now all I have to do is outline the results of my research in a logical, sequential order. In doing that, a picture should emerge. And along with the picture will come a clarity that I hope proves cathartic. So here we go, buckle up. It's going to be a bumpy ride.

2

Even at this early stage, the writing process is proving more challenging than I imagined. Committing words to paper somehow makes what happened seem all the more real. That may seem ridiculous to some, but it's true. I knew the writing would be demanding, but not this demanding. I worry the process cements memories that a part of me still fears were best left in the past.

After a few drinks, I came close to deleting the manuscript entirely. But after a lengthy, and at times, somewhat heated discussion with my wife, I finally decided to continue for all the reasons that I started in the first place. Nicola – that's my wife's name – has become increasingly frustrated by my prevarication and inconsistency. I think she may see this project as my last chance to save our relationship. She hasn't actually said that, not in so many words, but there's a growing distance between us that tells its own story. Nicola cried during our conversation, silent tears staining her pretty features, her eyes reddening, the tell-tale signs of stress changing the contours of her face. I'd spent many weeks telling her why this book was of crucial importance, persuading her to that end, asking for her patience and support, which she readily offered, as is her nature. And then there I was, contradicting my impassioned arguments. I can understand her frustration. *Why wouldn't she be agitated? Why wouldn't she be exasperated?* Amazingly, she hasn't given up on me altogether. At one point, Nicola even knelt at my feet as I sat on the sofa. That made me feel so very uncomfortable, realising the depth of her feelings, knowing I'd let her down. She placed an open hand on each of my knees, looking up into my eyes, pleading with me to see through what I'd started. I'd never seen her so passionate, never so desperate, and it touched my heart, giving me the strength to carry on.

'You *have* to defeat your demons, Anthony, for you, for me, and for our little girl.'

I averted my eyes to the wall, nodding once as she continued.

'You've told me that the writing of this book is the only way you're ever going to find peace. You've said little else for weeks on end. And I've listened, I've taken you seriously, finally accepting your arguments.'

She increased her grip, digging in her nails, grabbing my attention.

'And now, when you've finally made a start, you're ready to give up on it. It would be best if you kept going, Anthony. Things can't carry on as they are.'

She only ever calls me Anthony to drive a point home when something *really* matters to her, when things are serious. I took a deep breath, sucking in the air and swallowing my doubts, forcing them back down my throat rather than say something I knew she didn't want to hear. I nodded again, more forcibly, this time with a jerk of my head, manufacturing a smile that I suspect was far from convincing. I told her that I'd keep writing, stating it with passion, the words, pitch and tone intended to convince her of my commitment to our family.

I love Nicola so very much, and our daughter Olivia, too. Continuing my story is the least I can do. I couldn't guarantee I'd get to the end of the process; that would have been dishonest. But I did promise to do my very best. And I meant it, too, every word of it. So, I've taken a month's leave from work, four whole weeks, to get the book moving. I've converted the spare bedroom at the back of the house into a home office. And I'm planning to spend several hours a day putting words on the page.

And I'll get on with it, determination silencing my deep anxiety and dread. There's no avoiding the trepidation. But I won't let that hold me back. What happened, happened. I can only tell it as it was. That's the point of it all, the truth and nothing but the truth.

3

I've spent many hours interviewing my mother, father and sister. And they were *interviews* rather than conversations. I asked the questions, and they answered. I pushed them on subjects that were hard for them to discuss. That may seem harsh given our close familial relationships, but it was the only way to facilitate the process effectively.

I even recorded our meetings and made written notes, as I would at work for an article. I'm keen not to misrepresent anything any of the three said. None of them found our interactions easy, and that's putting it mildly. My family were such a big part of what happened, for good or bad.

At this stage of the writing process, I think it makes sense to fully explain how I came to encounter Dr Galbraith. A series of events led to our unfortunate meeting. That's how life is sometimes, wrong place, wrong time, and the results can be dire.

My father had an affair with a woman he worked with at a local bank. My mother had her suspicions – he was working late a little too often, there was lipstick on a shirt collar, the hint of unfamiliar perfume – and then she caught them together one lunchtime at a local restaurant. They were holding hands across the table.

That's how it started. My family's seemingly happy life was blown apart. My mother and father had been childhood sweethearts. They married young and had two children together. And yet, despite all that, he let her down, not because of love but due to lust. Those are his words, not mine. It was all about sex. A driving force that features in my story all too often in one way or another. My father was thinking with his dick.

But my father didn't just have an affair; he left the family home, moving in with Tina, a much younger woman, or 'the tart', as my mother chose to call her. Both the heated arguments before my father's leaving, and even more so the going itself, had a profound impact on my psychological and emotional wellbeing. We'd been close, my father and me. The man was my hero. Though, looking back, I don't think he'd done a great deal to deserve that accolade, other than being there.

Nonetheless, the separation hit me hard. I blamed myself for his leaving, as young children often do. My sister was less affected. As a teenager, she'd better understood that his departure had nothing to do with her. And, in her own words, friends and what they thought often seemed more important than family back then. But it wasn't that way for me. My world became a darker place. My mother tried her very best to alleviate my anxiety. She was understanding, patient and affectionate. She explained time and again that my father leaving was his doing and his alone. That he still loved me as he had before. That his feelings for me hadn't changed.

But nothing she said or did made any difference to my sense of abandonment. I thought I must have done something truly awful to deserve such a fate. I regressed, causing her a great deal of worry at an already difficult time. I became abusive, not physically but verbally, telling the poor woman I hated her more than once. I didn't, of course, those weren't my true feelings, but I'd said it. My mother was an easy target. And so, she was on the receiving end. She didn't deserve that. It's something I regret to this day.

* * *

As I interviewed my mother for the first time, she talked of those dark times with sadness, still experiencing unjustified feelings of guilt for the part she played in leading me to Galbraith's door. I told her she was simply doing what she'd thought was best. That she couldn't possibly have known what the man was or what he did. But my well-meaning words of reassurance made no more difference than hers had all those years ago. My mother, like myself, wishes she could rewrite the past. That was clear from her countenance, her words, her body language. But, of course, such things aren't possible.

I asked her to describe the sequence of events that led to that first meeting with the doctor who changed everything. She sighed deeply, repeatedly tapping a foot against the kitchen floor as she sipped her peppermint tea. And then, after a moment of contemplative silence, my mother began talking in a faltering voice that betrayed her mood. This is an accurate record of our conversation taken from my notes.

'It was a difficult time, Tony, so very difficult. Your father had left us to live with that young tart he'd met at work. Your sister was playing up in the way teenagers often do, experimenting with alcohol and drugs, staying out late at night, not telling me where she was going, who she was with, or even when she was coming back. And you were finding the changes in our life incredibly hard to deal with; even your teacher was concerned. She told me as much. She said you'd regressed. I didn't even know what the word meant at the time. I had to look it up. It was as if you were three or four again. Like we'd gone back in time. You were wetting the bed, sucking your thumb. I don't think you remember how bad things had got.'

I shook my head. 'I remember more than you realise.'

She looked less than persuaded. 'Do you, *really*?'

'Yes, I do. Some things stuck in my mind.'

'You started taking a teddy bear to bed each night as you had as a toddler. Mr Snuggles, you even gave the bear a name. And you weren't going out to play with your friends. You'd stopped going to rugby training, anything to avoid mixing with other people. That *really* did worry me. You know how much you loved rugby. It had been such a big part of our life until then. I tried talking to your father; I asked him to spend more time with you. I told him you were missing him terribly and how it was affecting you, but he had other things on his mind. He was in a new relationship. He seemed obsessed with the girl, and we'd become less of a priority.

'Your gran was living in Spain. I'd speak to her on the phone, but that wasn't the same as talking face to face. She wasn't there for me when I needed her most. Not as she had been before the move. And Gramps was ill. He was getting weaker. She had enough to deal with without my problems. I'd never felt more alone.'

'I do know it can't have been easy for you.'

It wasn't something I'd ever thought about before, the events of that time as they affected her. But when I spoke those words, I meant them. I felt genuine empathy for my mother as she continued talking, the past reaching out to sink its claws into her, beating her down as it does me.

'Easy is the last thing it was. I knew you needed help, and so did I. I had to do something. You do understand that, don't you? What would you have done in my place? What if it was Olivia we were talking about? You were so clingy, so tearful, so prone to tantrums. What other choice did I have?'

I reached out, squeezing my mother's hand as she stalled, lowering her gaze to the floor.

'It's okay, Mum. I know you had my best interests at heart. Please keep talking. I want to hear your side of things. It may even prove cathartic for you too. What happened next?'

She blew the air from her mouth.

'I kept hoping things would get better as the days passed, but they didn't. If anything, they got even worse. I'd been toying with the idea of seeking professional help. I'd read something in a woman's magazine at the hairdresser, the problems page. Someone had written to the agony aunt in very similar circumstances. And then, one day, everything came to a head. You'd peed the bed again, you'd hidden the soiled bedclothes in your wardrobe, and then that same morning, you threw an entire bowl of cereal across the kitchen before bursting into a flood of tears. There was one hell of a mess. I was clinging on by my fingernails by that point. It was more than I could take.'

I had a vague recollection of those events, but no more than that. 'Why would I do that?' I said.

'It was a Friday morning. Your father rang me, cancelling his access visit that coming weekend. He had something else on. I had to tell you he wasn't coming. The new woman in his life was more important than we were. I didn't say that, of course, not the last bit. I made something up to soften the blow. But that was the reality. You'd been so looking forward to seeing him. You'd been talking about it all week. Building it up in your mind. You took the news so very hard. You couldn't put it into words, so you acted out. And it felt like you blamed me.'

'Oh, shit, that all makes sense. Shoot the messenger; I was angry with him but took it out on you.'

She nodded her agreement.

'I was mentally and physically exhausted by then. I couldn't cope with any more. That morning felt like the last straw.'

'I thought it was my fault, all of it, his leaving, going off with someone new. I thought it was all down to me. I've read about it – the theory – that's what young kids do. They think the whole world revolves around them.'

'I told you it wasn't your fault. I kept telling you.' My mother began crying, not an easy thing for me to witness, but I guess an inevitable part of the process. It was – stop the interview or continue; I decided on the latter.

'I didn't believe you.'

'I was sinking, Tony; I couldn't have done more. I did my best.'

'I know you did, Mum, I know.'

'Really?'

'Yes, *really!*'

She smiled without parting her lips; the tension mitigated for a fleeting moment as my simple words of reassurance eased her angst.

'That's good to hear. Maybe there's some point to this after all.'

I spoke slowly, clearly enunciating each word, keen to keep her talking. 'Okay, let's move on. I get that you needed help. No one could blame you for that. And I certainly don't. But how did all that lead to my seeing Galbraith?'

Mum stared into the distance, travelling back in time.

'We all saw him, me, you, Dad and Siân.'

'Yes, I remember, but how did it come about?'

She sighed again, the tension back. 'I wasn't coping, Tony. I talked to Dr Proctor, our GP – you must remember her.'

I nodded my confirmation, waiting for my mother to continue as I knew she inevitably would. She'd started, so she'd finish. There was purpose in the telling.

'I thought the doctor might prescribe you something, you know, to calm you down a bit until you came to terms with the changes in our lives. But she recommended the child guidance clinic. She was persuasive. She assured me it had a good reputation. It seemed like a good idea. What more can I say? It was a relief, to be honest. I thought you were going to get the help you needed. I talked to Gran on the phone, and she thought the same thing. It wasn't just me.'

'What about Dad?'

I hadn't meant anything by it. It was a straightforward query to establish the facts. There was no implied criticism. But I think my mother took it that way. Straight on the defensive, she snapped out her reply.

'What do you mean?'

'Well, what did Dad think? It's a simple enough question.'

She rolled her eyes, her expression hardening. She may well have regretted agreeing to be interviewed at all, then. I can't be sure.

'Oh, here we go again. I'm always the bad guy. You've got to blame someone, so why not me? Is that it? Is that where this is going?'

I leant towards her, considering her three questions in one, all meaning the same thing. All coming from the same place.

'That is *not* what I'm thinking, Mum. Maybe when I was a child, yes, but certainly not now. I want to know the facts, that's all, for the sake of the story. There's no blame, definitely not from me.'

'If you're sure?'

'I've never been more sure.'

I'd said it with conviction, meaning every word.

She didn't respond, sitting in silence.

I cleared my throat, not willing to let it go. I'd committed to honesty, warts and all. I need that from others too. 'So, Dad, what did he think about the clinic idea? He must have had an opinion.'

My mother still seemed reluctant to answer, but then, all of a sudden, the words poured from her mouth as if in a torrent. 'He didn't like the idea. There, I've said it. Are you happy now? Is that what you wanted to hear? But don't go thinking your father was anything other than selfish. He didn't want his dirty washing aired in public, that's all. He knew *all* our problems were down to him. Talking about it was the last thing he wanted, and particularly to a stranger.'

'But he ended up going along with it.'

'Yes, he did, after some persuasion.'

'I remember.'

'Do you?'

'As if it were yesterday.'

She pressed her lips together.

'I'm tired, Tony. That's enough for today.'

I hid my disappointment as best I could and contemplated talking her into continuing, but I decided against it. I had to consider her feelings. It's not all about me.

'Okay, we can speak together again in a day or two.'

My mother rose to her feet a little unsteadily, shifting her weight from one foot to the other. She's not as strong as she once was. Time hasn't been kind and the events of our shared past took an inevitable toll. I hadn't realised quite how much until now.

'I wish I'd never heard of that clinic. You do realise that, don't you, Tony?'

'Of course I do.'

She turned her back to me, approaching the fridge. 'Are you

stopping for something to eat? I've got some nice vegetable casserole left over from yesterday's tea if you fancy it? I could heat it up with some rice.'

I shook my head, keen to get out of there. I wanted to check my notes, listen to the recording. Eating could wait.

'I'd better get off,' I said. 'Nicola will be waiting for me.'

My mother followed me down the hall as I approached the front door. 'Are you certain this book's a good idea, Tony?'

It hadn't been an easy conversation for either of us. As I turned to nod, forcing a thin smile, I tried to look a lot more convinced than I felt.

'It's something I've got to do, please accept that. It's my only hope of coming to terms with the past. Maybe then, when it's done, I can look to the future. It's not something I'm doing on a whim. I've been thinking about it for months.'

'If you're sure?'

'I'm sure.'

I decided to call at a local pub on my way home – just for the one beer. I was driving, after all. But I think it was justified. A drink sometimes settles my nerves.

4

Galbraith produced videos of the many abominations he inflicted on his young victims in a white-tiled cellar hidden below the large Georgian townhouse he shared with his wife and two young daughters. I haven't had the misfortune of viewing all those vile films, for which I'll be eternally grateful, but I've talked to a police officer who has.

She was a young detective constable at the time, part of the county's child protection services, but she's far more senior now. She's asked me not to reveal her rank for fear of being identified; she wants no further press interest or attention. There was more than enough of that at the time.

The poor woman told me that her involvement in the case had emotionally scarred her for life, that she'll never forget the horrors she witnessed. But she'd had no choice but to sit there watching the unwatchable, one awful video after another, identifying child victims and offenders where possible, and listing the many offences, on one particularly foul occasion, even murder.

The officer winced as she told me of that snuff film. A young, chestnut-brown-haired boy of about my age at that time, shackled to a white-tiled wall, being beaten by two naked men wearing nothing but black leather bondage hoods with slits for their eyes, noses and mouths. Galbraith was one of the two men, he appeared in all his videos, but the other man remains unidentified despite the police's best efforts to find him.

The officer was close to tears as she described the murder scene, the boy hanging bruised and bleeding from thin twisted arms, intermingling body fluids pooling around his feet as the men's many blows increased in severity. I could see the officer tense, her expression tortured as she clenched her hands into tight fists, raising her eyes to the ceiling as if bemoaning humanity's many failings. She shook her head to the left and right on rising to her feet moments later, wiping her eyes with the back of one hand as she approached a large picture window with a view of the police headquarters car park three floors below.

The officer continued speaking with her back to me, stalling more than once to swallow her sadness. It was clear the memories still stung. Time had softened their impact only slightly, if at all.

'It wasn't only the films that were found. Galbraith kept detailed, alphabetically ordered records of everything he did to his many victims. He noted the nature of each act of depravity and the effect it had on each child. It was as if he thought he was carrying out a legitimate scientific study. It reminded me of some terrible things I'd read about the Nazi death camps, monsters like Mengele. He was a doctor, too. I really don't think Galbraith fully appreciated the heinous nature of what he was doing.'

I shook my head incredulously. 'Oh, come on, he was an intelligent man, an academic. *Surely,* you're not trying to say he wasn't fully culpable for his actions.'

She was quick to reply. 'Oh God, no! Don't get me wrong, I'm not saying he didn't *know* he was harming those boys. His notes make it perfectly clear that he did. I've no doubt he *revelled* in their suffering. He was a total psycho, evil personified, the worst criminal I've ever had the misfortune to encounter in a very long career. But I believe he thought his criminal acts were justified. He thought he was better than those children, that they didn't matter, that his needs came first. The man really was that deluded. He was a sadist, the very definition of a predator, who had access to vulnerable children, and he took full advantage. He thought of no one but himself. Only he mattered, just his needs and his alone, whatever the cost to others.'

'His job gave him access to victims. Do you think that happened by accident?'

The officer emitted a sharp laugh that had nothing to do with humour. 'Galbraith was a planner, a schemer. Nothing happened unless he meant it to. That's how he got away with his crimes for as long as he did. His entire life was geared towards his evil desires. I've no doubt he worked with children to facilitate his offending. Abusing kids and getting away with it? It's what he lived for.'

I indicated my agreement. She'd put it so well. That was my understanding too. In some strange way, I took satisfaction in that.

* * *

As we continued talking, a genuinely horrible realisation dawned. She told me of an interview she'd conducted with an abused boy, one who'd mentioned both a white room and an abusive doctor. She went on to talk of information received by the police, not only suggesting that an organised paedophile ring was operating in the area, but that Galbraith was an active member. I checked the dates, once, then again, shaken by my discovery. All that happened *before* I was the focus of Galbraith's depraved attentions. The police already had the evidence she'd outlined at the time he was targeting me.

If only, if only! I could have screamed. *But what was the point in even thinking it? What happened, happened.* I fought to retain my composure, insisting I needed to know more. She said things weren't nearly as simple as they appeared. It seems to me they seldom are.

I pressed the officer for further information but without success. For whatever reason, to my huge frustration, she decided she'd said enough.

* * *

We arranged a second meeting for the next day, when she said she'd have more time to discuss the case. She also recommended I speak to another police officer named Pam Forsyth and an ex-child protection social work manager named Mel Nicholson. Both, she said, could tell me more, which would help me make sense of events. The reasons for police inaction prior to my first appointment at the clinic would become clear.

I found her assertion very hard to believe or accept. As I sat there, searching for the words to express my anger and confusion, she smiled, her face softening, a side of her I hadn't seen before. I opened my mouth as if to speak, but all was silence. She crossed the room, switching on a green plastic kettle on a small table opposite her desk. 'Coffee?'

I wanted to shout, to stamp my feet, to demand she tell me more, not the next day, but then. It seemed she did have time after all. I still think I should have been more insistent. But instead, I nodded, reluctantly accepting that further clarification would have to wait.

'Strong, black, with one sugar, please,' I said, hoping having coffee with her would loosen her tongue. 'I'm on a bit of a diet. I've cut down from two.'

She poured the boiling water, added instant coffee and a single spoonful of white sugar before stirring.

'And a biscuit?'

I refused with thanks, patting my belly. In reality, I was feeling nauseous, my gut twisting, the stress getting to me. But I said I didn't want to spoil my appetite, that I was meeting Cynthia at a café in town, another interview planned.

The officer raised an eyebrow. 'Cynthia Galbraith?'

'Yes, although it's Cynthia Jones these days. It took a bit of effort to find her, but she's finally agreed to talk to me.'

The officer sat back down, raising her mug to her lips, drinking before placing it back on her desk. I could see her left eye twitching ever so slightly as she spoke. 'I'm not sure I would have in her place.'

'I'm just glad the interview's happening. She was married to the man, lived in the same house, bore his children. She's a big part of the story. I'll be interested to hear what she has to say.'

I checked my high-end Swiss watch, received as an overly generous Christmas gift from Nicola the previous year. The minutes were ticking by, and it was time to go. It seemed obvious the officer wasn't going to return to our previous conversation nor appreciate the distress her information had caused me. I don't think the significance of the dates hit her as it did me.

I confirmed our meeting for the following day before leaving, and she smiled for a second time, waving as I left the room.

5

I seriously considered rearranging my interview with Cynthia, given the upset caused by my visit to police headquarters. My head was aching, I wasn't in the best of moods, and I needed a drink. But I told myself to focus on the task at hand, that she might not be so cooperative again if I cancelled.

There were a lot of things I wanted to ask Cynthia, things I needed to know. And those questions came to mind now as I made my journey through the familiar town I call home. What drew her into Galbraith's clutches? Why did she marry such a man? Why did she stay with him for as long as she did? Did she know what he was from the start? Or was his true nature a revelation to her too? These were things only Cynthia could clarify. I hoped she'd explain all of that and tell me more about the deviant doctor too, how he operated, the methods he used to con and control. I needed to understand.

Cynthia and Galbraith were together for several years. She must have had a deeper knowledge of his characteristics and qualities than almost anyone else on earth.

* * *

I parked in a convenient spot in the main street, about a five-minute brisk walk from the café, before hurrying along the pavement with quick-moving feet, increasing my pace as a cold winter drizzle began to fall, dampening everything in its path. I entered Merlin's Lane at just before one o'clock that afternoon, arriving at the door of the popular vegetarian eatery a couple of minutes later than intended. I was very much hoping Cynthia would be there waiting for me when I opened the door, which thankfully she was. She hadn't backed out, which to some extent surprised me. I saw her sitting at the back of the orange-painted room almost as soon as I entered, recognising her from photos I'd seen on social media.

Cynthia looked a little older than she had in the online images, a middle-aged woman with caramel-blonde hair, a few pounds heavier than she had been, and wearing an olive-green wool jumper and faded blue jeans, which for some reason, I noted suited her well. She looked comfortable in her own skin, if a little anxious.

In the unusual circumstances, who wouldn't be nervous? I'm sure she saw the same in me. She stood, smiling thinly as I approached her table, close to the café's serving counter. We shook hands for a fraction of a second longer than was comfortable before we both sat, opposite each other.

She had a half-full cup of herbal tea on the table in front of her. I hadn't been to the café before, the location of our meeting was her choice, not mine. But I liked the place immediately. There were paintings and photographs by local artists covering three of the four walls, which I found appealing. In other circumstances, I'd have had a good time. But I was there to work, not to enjoy the convivial atmosphere. The ambience wasn't lost on me, but it was far from a priority.

We chatted for a few awkward minutes, ordering snacks; time passed slowly until I began the interview process. Cynthia appeared keen to talk once we'd started. I got the distinct impression that she wanted to tell her story. She wanted me to understand and for others to understand too. Galbraith had touched both our lives.

As I sat there, looking across the table at this ordinary but attractive woman, I reminded myself of the need to keep an open mind, not to make assumptions, and to conduct the interview professionally, as I would any other. Easier said than done; I had my inevitable prejudices. I found myself thinking that she must have been at least partly responsible for Galbraith's ongoing offending. I felt a degree of resentment towards her, even anger, which I struggled to control. Surely it was reasonable to apply a modicum of blame.

* * *

I took a notepad and pen from my black leather briefcase a few seconds before a waitress delivered our orders to the table, a toasted cheese and tomato sandwich for me and vegetable soup for Cynthia. She declined the offer of bread.

We talked as we ate, me asking the questions and her answering, much as I had done with my family. I made intermittent notes, putting down my sandwich and picking up a biro as required. I didn't record the interview this time due to the invasive chatter emanating from other nearby tables. It just wasn't practical.

As Cynthia answered each of my questions in turn, with what I considered openness and honesty, I came to realise that she was a victim, too. Galbraith was an arch manipulator, a predator at the very top of his game. He lied, he twisted, and he schemed. Cynthia was on the receiving end of his wicked attention, as I was. In many ways, we were the same.

Cynthia first encountered Galbraith at the age of eighteen, when he was a visiting lecturer at her university in Cardiff. He was aware of her, more than she was of him.

Unknown to Cynthia, the doctor had already targeted her by the time they first met. He'd planned it from the start. I asked her how she could possibly know that for sure. She had a pained expression on her face when she gave me her answer.

'Oh, he left me in no doubt. It was all part of his game. He told me all about it towards the end of our relationship when mocking my decline. It amused him to upset me. The more distressed I became, the happier he was. It was something he was good at. He revelled in whatever distress he caused. It filled him with joy. Hurting me, humiliating me, became a daily ritual, it never stopped.'

I listened with interest and the more Cynthia said, speaking between her tears, the clearer it all became. Galbraith broke her, minute by minute, hour by hour, day by day. He did it because he enjoyed it, because it aroused him, because he could. And he made a written record of that process too. She was a case study, just like the unfortunate boys shackled to the wall in that white-tiled cellar. And just like me.

The interview was proving more informative than I could ever have hoped, one revelation and insight after another. Once Cynthia started talking, it seemed she couldn't stop. And as she spoke, all my earlier prejudices were melting away.

'Why did Galbraith choose you to target? Of all the young women at the university, why pick you out?'

She sighed deeply, lowering her gaze. 'He never told me, and I didn't ask. Maybe it was simply that I was dating a boy he taught. Or maybe he saw a vulnerability in me, a naivety he could use to his advantage. I've thought about it a lot over the years, but I've never come up with a satisfactory answer. I'm finally resigned to the fact it's something I'm never going to know.'

Cynthia wept as she told me of her first love, Steven, a fellow student, with whom she'd cohabited in her first year in Cardiff. The young man was studying psychology. Galbraith was one of his tutors. The loving couple had visited the pleasant Pembrokeshire seaside town of Tenby to stay with Cynthia's parents, Steven meeting them for the first time. Cynthia described events leading to the trip at length. But I was keen to move the conversation along. That's not something I'm proud of, and I'm sure my tone betrayed my impatience. She was talking of things that mattered to her. I should have given her more time. That seems to be becoming a theme – something I'll need to keep an eye on if I'm to be a better person.

'Was there any particular relevance to your trip to Tenby?'

She lowered her eyes again, a pinched expression on her face as if reliving times gone by. 'Steven was the love of my life. We were only together a short time, but I still think of him that way. Tenby was the end of it all.'

'I don't understand.'

Cynthia's face paled, her brow furrowed. She was silent for a second or two. I didn't rush her this time, allowing her to tell her story at her own pace. 'We were staying at my parents' house. Steven went out running. It was something he did most days. But this time was different. He didn't come back.'

I raised a hand to my chin. 'What happened?'

'Steven was hit by a car on the seafront. He died there on the road – hit and run. I didn't know at the time, but Galbraith ran him over. He'd followed him and it was no accident. He saw Steven jogging along that dark winter street; he ensured there were no witnesses, looking from left to right, checking his mirrors. And then, when he thought the time was precisely right, he pressed his foot down hard on the accelerator. He mounted the pavement, hitting Steven full-on, sending him sprawling over the bonnet. His skull cracked against the road, fractured. I've pictured that scene what must be a thousand times. It's imprinted on my mind, never to be forgotten. It was murder. The bastard killed Steven as if his life was worthless. I hated him for that. I still do.'

I wondered if her tale was more imagination than truth, and it seemed Cynthia could sense my doubt.

She let out a groan. 'David told me, he gave me every detail, years later, when he thought it would maximise my suffering. That's what he did. He told me the story as I told it to you. Although he took pleasure in the telling. He wasn't worried I'd go to the police. The dead can't speak, and he planned to kill me too.'

I pushed my plate aside, making some hurried written notes in scribbled blue script.

'I'm sorry for your loss.'

She acknowledged my empathetic response with a slight nod of her head. 'It was a long time ago.'

'So, take me back to the beginning, how did you first meet Galbraith? Was it at the university?'

She shook her head.

'I, er, I met him at Steven's funeral. That was no accident either; David had planned that, too. He approached me as I left the Narberth crematorium, in the car park. I remember him touching my arm very briefly and smiling. He introduced himself as Dr Galbraith, one of Steven's lecturers, and said he was so very sorry for my loss, much as you did. But, of course, my emotions were far more heightened back then. He understood that, taking full advantage. He extolled Steven's virtues, saying he was a wonderful young man, that he'd miss him terribly, that his death was a tragedy that was hard to bear. He was charm personified. And, do you know, I actually liked him? That's what the bastard did; he manipulated everyone around him, skilfully and deliberately. He wormed his way in, and he was good at it, too, something of an expert. He had me conned from the very start. I saw through him in the end, of course. But that took time. A lot longer than you'd imagine.'

Cynthia had me fascinated now. I wanted to know more. 'What happened next?'

'David wrote to me while I was still staying with my parents before the start of the next term.'

'A letter?'

She let out a snort of disdain, spitting her words from her mouth. 'Written in his usual flowing copperplate script, intended to impress. He didn't do anything without reason. Everything had a purpose.'

'Tell me more.'

She drained her cup, ordering another chamomile tea with a twist of lemon. 'I was studying law, but I couldn't face going back. David began the process of persuading me not only to return to university but to change my course to psychology. He used my love of Steven against me. I was vulnerable, grieving, and David knew that. He told me that changing my course was what Steven would have wanted. He told me to think of it as a tribute to my lost love.'

'And did you? Change your course, I mean?'

She looked up, smiling as a young waitress with bright blue hair delivered her order to the table. Cynthia waited for the girl to walk away with a sway of her hips before returning her attention to me. 'Where were we?'

'You were about to tell me if you changed your course.'

'Not then, not initially, that took some persuading. But David got what he wanted in the end. He usually did. He made sure of that, one way or another.'

'How?' It was the only thing I could think to ask.

'David arranged to meet me a week or two later, there in Tenby, on the pretext that he was visiting an ageing relative in the area. He came to the house, met my parents, who thought he was wonderful, and then took me out for an evening meal at a local Indian restaurant I was particularly fond of. Not a date, you understand, he was there as my adviser. He'd said the purpose of the evening was to discuss my academic future, but, of course, unknown to me, he had his own deviant goals in mind. I was to be part of the false picture of respectability he presented to the world. The mask behind which he hid. And he had plans to break my spirit, study my decline. He was playing the long game. I was a lab rat caught in his trap, no more important to him than that.'

I was beginning to understand the lengths to which Galbraith was prepared to go to achieve whatever aim he had in mind. He was no opportunist, no ordinary criminal. 'How did the evening go? Please tell me everything. I've got as long as it takes.'

'David plied me with strong drink while remaining sober himself. I think that sums it up. That was the foundation of his plan. It didn't have to be complex, sometimes simple schemes were the most effective. He did whatever worked best in the particular circumstances.

'And he talked of Steven, Steven's love of psychology, and my responsibility to honour his memory. He set the scene at the funeral, and then it was more of the same. I guess it was a little like being brainwashed. We were in the restaurant for over two hours, and he didn't stop talking, driving his message home, shaping my thoughts. David wanted me back in Cardiff, studying under his tutelage. It was all part of his plan. And I was sucked right in. I don't think I ever stood a chance. Another letter arrived a few days later.'

'Saying what?'

'I'd agreed to change courses, apparently.'

'And had you?'

She shook her head, pensive. 'I really don't think so. But I was very drunk that night. He'd made certain of that. I couldn't be sure. And the letter made it clear he'd already made the necessary arrangements. He'd spoken to my law professor, completed the necessary paperwork on my behalf; it was a done deal. And David was to be my mentor. I was to live rent-free in a student property he owned in Cardiff, a shared house, or so he told me, although my supposed fellow students didn't exist in reality. And he was to visit me weekly to offer support, to help me catch up with the aspects of the new course I'd missed. I wasn't overly pleased. It all felt so out of my control. But Mum and Dad were encouraging. They saw it all as nothing but positive. In the end, a part of me started to think a new start might not be such a bad idea after all.'

I was beginning to better appreciate just how Machiavellian Galbraith was. My knowledge was growing. The doctor was cunning, scheming, unscrupulous. I saw his face in my mind's eye, blinking it away. 'The bastard was in control.'

Cynthia nodded. 'I found myself living alone in that house. The other students were always *about* to turn up but never did. I became more isolated, withdrawn, working hard, getting good grades, but doing little else. David would turn up once a week, when he'd inspect every inch of the place, complimenting me on what he said I'd done well and criticising anything he saw as my failings. There were always criticisms. The place had to be immaculate, every inch of it. All the food cans in the kitchen cupboards had to be facing forwards and in order of size, large to the left, smaller to the right. He'd use a ruler to ensure the gaps between the cans were the same. And he'd use a white cotton glove to examine surfaces for signs of dust, on shelves, on top of doors, even the top of the fridge, everywhere. He'd give me marks out of ten as he went from room to room. I dreaded those visits, his disapproval, the inevitable snide remarks. But he could be charming too when it suited him. When it served his purpose.'

I checked my watch. 'Can you give me an example?'

'Are you pushed for time?'

I shook my head. 'No, no, not at all, although I'll need to ring my wife in half an hour or so. She'll need to collect our daughter from school.'

'How old is she?'

'She's four.'

Cynthia smiled warmly, her face softening. 'A lovely age, although I was so very pleased when mine grew up.'

I thought it was an odd thing for her to say, but I didn't comment. I needed her to focus back on the story. 'You were telling me about your life in Cardiff. You said that Galbraith could be charming as well as critical.'

'Yes, when it suited him, but the emphasis was usually on criticism. He wanted me desperate for his approval. It gave him his power. He was like a puppet master, pulling my strings, making me dance.'

'How bad did it get?'

'I can't begin to explain it.'

'I'd be grateful if you'd try.'

She exhaled slowly, gripping the edge of the table with both hands, her knuckles white. 'There was that one night. He'd isolated me from friends by that stage, and my family thought he could do no wrong. He'd filled their heads with lies, using my grief against me. He'd convinced them not to believe a single word I said of any potential significance without checking the facts with him. They saw him as my saviour. I thought of leaving at times, but I had nowhere to go. And, to be brutally honest, I don't think I'd have had the confidence to escape, whatever my options. I really was that low. He'd crushed what little self-esteem I had left. Any decision was difficult, even about the most mundane daily things, let alone something as important as my wellbeing and safety. His constant disapproval had got worse. The state of the house wasn't ever good enough, despite hours of cleaning. And my grades were never up to his required standard, whatever my other lecturers said. He often said I was failing Steven's memory, that I'd let him down.

'And then, that particular evening, David arrived at the house in an unusually positive mood. I'd never seen him so cheerful. There were none of his usual criticisms, no snide remarks. He took me out to a lovely local Italian restaurant where all the staff knew him by name. They all liked him, or so it seemed. He was charming, complimentary, and he got me drunk again, as he had that time in Tenby. And then, when we got back to the house, he continued chatting about opera, art, and music, with apparent warmth and enthusiasm. I actually began enjoying his company. I can't believe I'm saying that, but it's true. It was almost as if he was a different person, the charmer I'd met at the crematorium. But then things took a terrible turn.'

'Please, what happened?'

'I went to the bathroom. I'd drunk a lot of wine. I needed the toilet. He handed me another drink as soon as I returned to the lounge, brandy, in a crystal glass, no doubt meant to flatter and impress. And that's the last thing I remember of that night. I was in terrible pain when I woke the next morning. There was blood on my bedsheets, multiple deep scratch marks on my body, mainly on my back and buttocks but in other places too. I remember standing, peering over my shoulder, looking at myself naked in a full-length mirror on the back of the wardrobe door. I was scared, trembling, close to panic. I had no idea what had happened. I couldn't remember a thing. None of it made any sense at all. When I went to challenge him, to ask for an explanation, to try to make sense of events, I found he'd already left the house.'

'Did you go to the police?'

I regretted the question almost as soon as I asked it. Cynthia pressed herself against the back of her seat, shoulders slumped over her chest as if trying to make herself smaller. If the floor had opened, she'd have jumped right in. When she spoke, her voice was faltering.

'I should have, I know I should have, but he... he had such domination over me, such power. It's hard to explain it properly, but I want you to understand. I was a shadow of my former self, completely under his control. David's word was law. When I did get the chance to talk to him, he acted as if I was making a fuss about nothing. I remember him laughing hysterically when I expressed my concerns. I felt so stupid, so ridiculous. He made out we'd enjoyed a wild night of sexual passion, that I'd willingly consented, even that I'd taken the lead, seducing him with my feminine wiles, stripping for his entertainment, not taking no for an answer. But I didn't see him that way. He was so much older than me. I was baffled, perplexed. I couldn't make sense of any of it. I didn't trust my own mind. I realise now that the bastard had drugged me. Looking back, it seems obvious. It couldn't be more obvious. But I didn't see it at the time.'

'I'm sorry you had to go through that.'

'Oh, you haven't heard the half of it. It got worse. A few weeks later, I realised I was pregnant.'

'Galbraith?'

'Oh, yes, I can say that with absolute certainty. I was a virgin when I met Steven. There was just Steven, and then David. I hadn't had sex with anyone else.'

'How did Galbraith react when you mentioned the baby?'

'How do you think?'

I shook my head, unsure of how best to respond. I needed to hear it from her.

'Well, it wasn't in any way I'd expected, that's for sure. David said he was concerned about my mental health, that my nervousness wasn't good for the baby. He prescribed me anti-anxiety drugs, making me take them in line with his instructions. And then he insisted I leave my psychology course to focus on parenting. I protested; I wanted to finish my degree and look after the baby when the time came. But David argued I wasn't capable of both. He said it so many times and with such certainty that in the end, I believed him. That's typical of the influence he had over me. I ended up leaving Cardiff to live with him here in town.'

'At the house with the cellar?'

Cynthia raised a hand to her face, wiping away a tear. When she continued talking, she looked past me rather than meet my eyes. Her words were rushed, as if she wanted to get this part of her story over with as quickly as possible. As if the telling was hard to bear.

'David increased the strength of my tranquillisers very soon after the move. Taking them became a daily ritual he was keen to encourage. And then, when I was close to my due date, he suddenly announced that the medication would have a *terrible* physical impact on my unborn baby. My child would enter this world an addict, experiencing awful withdrawal symptoms: headaches, nausea, vomiting, stomach pains, cramps. Can you imagine? A newborn baby! My child would suffer from the first day of life. I was utterly devastated. I fell apart emotionally. David liked that. It amused him. I'd never felt so low. He'd insisted I take the damned medication. He always praised me when I swallowed a tablet. How could I possibly have known the implications? He was the doctor, the so-called expert. He called me a bad mother and repeated it often, sometimes screaming it in my face. "You're a bad mother already, Cynthia, bad, bad, *bad*! I hope you're ashamed of yourself."'

'That's truly awful!'

She screwed up her face. 'Shame became the mantra of my life, and then the worst thing of all... David told me that if the authorities ever found out I was such an incompetent mother, my baby would be taken away. I'd never see her again, not ever. He used that lie to control me, day after frightful day. You have to remember, David was a trained psychiatrist, a consultant, an expert in human behaviour. He saw everything from a Darwinian perspective, survival of the fittest. It was all a game to him, an experiment. I was dispensable, worthless, disposable, no more than that. His manipulations imprisoned me as effectively as any high prison walls. And who would have believed me over the esteemed Dr Galbraith, if I told them he'd pressured me to take the medicine?'

'What about the cellar?'

Her entire body tensed. 'I was hoping you wouldn't ask me about that.'

'It's an essential part of the story.'

She stiffened further. 'The cellar was David's territory, his domain, and entry was forbidden. I was ordered not to go down there under any circumstances.'

'Oh, come on, Cynthia, think about it. You lived in that house for several years. Galbraith and his like-minded criminals abused boys on the premises. The cellar was accessed via *your* kitchen. Surely you must have had *some* idea what was going on down there. Anything else isn't credible.'

Cynthia held her hands out in front of her, palms up. Everything about her conveyed her growing distress as she pleaded her case. 'I was drugged up constantly, beaten down by his constant physical and psychological abuse, incapable of independent thought. He told me the cellar was somewhere he saw patients.'

'And you believed him?'

'Yes, yes, for a long time, I did. I know that must seem ridiculous. I know I was in denial. I was refusing to see what was in front of my face. But I genuinely didn't understand what was going on. Please believe that. I'm not a bad person. David was evil. I'm nothing like him, not even close.'

I was tempted to push it, to challenge her further. But it was apparent she was struggling. It seemed advisable to leave it there. There was a real danger she'd shut down altogether if I pushed too hard, even walk out, leave the café. I'd come back to the cellar. It's an essential part of the story, horrible but vital. We would talk of it again. I was determined about that. But the timing had to be right.

* * *

'You had a second child?'

Cynthia relaxed slightly, her expression softening but only a little. She looked me in the eye now. 'Yes, another girl; he wanted a boy, of course, for obvious reasons I'm sure I don't need to explain. I thank God every day I didn't have one. Girls were of no interest to him. He saw our children as an inconvenience, no more than that. I remember his response when our second daughter was born. He called me useless, said that I couldn't even get that right. He never touched me again sexually after that, not even once, and I was glad of that. There was no affection in him, not for anyone but himself. He saw sex with me as an unfortunate necessity. A function he was forced to perform to create life. He was quite open about that. He took pleasure in the telling. I hate to think what fantasies he entertained to facilitate the physical act. He found all women repulsive. I'd just lie there, praying for it to be over.'

'But you stayed with him. Despite everything he did, despite everything he was.'

I hadn't meant my words to sound so accusatory, but they came out that way. I listened to her explanation with interest.

'David had convinced everyone that I was mentally ill – my GP, the health visitor, even my parents. They saw me as David's cross to bear. My mother actually used those words. I believed I'd lose my lovely girls if I ever left him. And I would have. He'd have ensured I did out of pure spite. And he'd have taken pleasure in doing it, too. Can you begin to imagine the life they'd have endured in his sole care? He was a hateful bastard. But everyone with any power over my life thought he was a wonderful man. I spit on his memory. The world would have been a better place had he never been born. If I could travel back in time to his birth, I'd happily smother the bastard myself. That one act would have saved so many people so much trauma. If only such things were possible. It's a fantasy I've indulged in more times than I care to count. What I went through was bad enough, but the children, oh God, the children. It breaks my heart to think of all the boys he harmed.'

I felt genuine sympathy for Cynthia as she told her story. Her sadness couldn't have been more evident. We talked for another ten minutes or so after that. About the likely impact on the many child victims rather than anything else. I would have liked to carry on talking about matters that related directly to me. But I could see she was tiring, clearly reluctant to say much more. I considered pushing her for more information but finally decided against. She'd had enough, that was obvious, and I needed to respect that. And sometimes piling on the pressure doesn't result in the desired outcome. Experience has taught me that. I was grateful that she agreed to a second interview to be arranged when I thought the time was right. I said I'd contact her, and she said that was fine. That she'd wait for my call. I did, however, have one final question before I left Cynthia that afternoon.

I asked her why she'd chosen the café as the venue for our meeting. It seemed a strange choice to me, given its very public nature. She told me it was somewhere she felt comfortable. That David Galbraith would have hated it, that he would never have eaten there, that the place had a bohemian vibe that wasn't his style. I liked the café even more after that. He'd left his mark on her as well.

I plan to return to the café someday in the not-too-distant future. With Nicola next time, to celebrate the completion of the book. There's an open mic night every Thursday evening at seven. That's the sort of thing Nicola enjoys. I'll try to look forward to that.

6

I was surprised and gratified when both Mel Nicholson and Pam Forsyth agreed to be interviewed without the need for a great deal of persuasion on my part. But neither could see me for several days, so I decided to use the time to interview Sharon Breen, Galbraith's former secretary. She was willing, she was available, so it seemed to make sense.

In all honesty, I questioned the value of interviewing Sharon before actually meeting her, but I couldn't have been more wrong. Our discussion, as hard to deal with as it undoubtedly was, was surprisingly informative once I'd had the chance to reflect on what she said. Sharon displayed a genuine hostility towards me from the first second to the last. It told me a lot about the doctor's persuasive powers, the skills with which he manipulated those around him, the mask behind which he hid to facilitate his crimes. Even after all the passing years and all the evidence, for Sharon, that mask was still very much in place.

I met Sharon early one evening at her semi-detached council house on the outskirts of town. She still works in admin, but for a local building firm these days, as opposed to the child guidance clinic of her younger years. She had a sour expression on her chubby face as she opened her front door. I could tell right from the very start that our meeting wouldn't be easy. I asked myself why she'd agreed to an interview at all.

Sharon led me into a faded but immaculate lounge, where she pointed towards a brown leather sofa, inviting me to sit. Her entire body wobbled like a birthday jelly as she sat her not inconsiderable bulk on a creaking armchair almost directly opposite me. A bad-tempered expression still dominated her features, making me question the wisdom of being there again. I could feel Sharon's loathing emanating from every pore. That's not an exaggeration; that's honestly how it felt. I thought she might actually hit me at one point. She had that look about her. As if she was having to hold herself back. By the time I took a notepad from my briefcase, she'd already told me I was wasting my time. For some reason I still can't comprehend, I decided to persevere rather than rush for the door.

* * *

'Thank you for agreeing to see me. I'm writing a book about my childhood experiences, as I explained on the phone. I was one of Dr Galbraith's patients at the age of seven. You worked closely with the doctor for several years. I'm hoping you can tell me how he conducted himself day to day. Did you get any clues as to the type of man he was? I remember that your office was immediately next to his. Any insights you can offer would be very much appreciated.'

Sharon sat there listening, wringing her hands together, contempt seeping from every inch of her. She blurted out her question as soon as I stopped speaking. 'Have you finished?'

I confirmed that I had, as she craned her neck towards me,

her face flushed, her wide-open eyes bulging as if they were about to pop from her head.

'Dr Galbraith was a good person, you know! He didn't do any of the awful things he was accused of. It was all lies! Dirty, filthy lies, every single word of it! And now here you are, dragging it all up again. You should be ashamed of yourself. You're a total disgrace. That's why I agreed to see you. I wanted to tell you that to your face.'

I have to admit I was taken aback by both the intensity and nature of her statement. It should have been blatantly obvious to me that nothing I could ever say would convince her of Galbraith's true nature. In some strange way, she's a victim, too. But her words hurt. I remember her being so very pleasant to me as a young patient. Now she was totally different. I spent the next five minutes or so outlining the wealth of evidence against Galbraith as she rocked in her seat, avoiding my gaze. I told her that many of the doctor's worst crimes were recorded on film, that he'd kept detailed notes, that there was no doubt about what he'd done. He was as guilty as sin. It really was that simple. But Sharon wasn't having any of it. The more I said, the angrier she got. Our meeting ended when she struggled to her feet, ordering me out of her house with a shake of a fist. She was still shouting abuse when I stepped out into the street.

'He was a lovely man, you lying bastard! He even bought me birthday presents! Did you hear that? Birthday fucking presents! How many bosses do that? You can fuck right off and die as far as I'm concerned. And as for your fucking book, I wouldn't wipe my arse with it.'

Galbraith still has his supporters, enthusiastic cheerleaders thirty years on. That surprised even me. Some find it easier to deny the truth. Sharon is one of those. And she's not the only one. No one will change that, not me or anyone else.

7

I've been talking to my dear wife about the progress of my writing. Although, to be more accurate, she did most of the talking and me the listening. I chose not to tell her of the distress caused by my recent interviews. I haven't fully processed the information gleaned myself yet. I'll choose my time to tell her when things are more straightforward in my mind.

Nicola watched a mildly entertaining TV quiz show in our family lounge while I put Olivia to bed at just after seven. I read my daughter a few paperback pages, Roald Dahl's *The Twits*, one of her favourites, pecked her gently on the cheek, and then lay at her side for a few minutes, keeping her company in the half-light until she was fast asleep and lost to her dreams. It's an evening ritual – something I love – a time I look forward to and cherish, as Olivia curls up safe and warm under her duck-down quilt. There's no threat to her there, no danger, and that puts my mind at rest, at least for a time. Another day has passed without her encountering a man like Galbraith. One of the monsters who lurk in the shadows, always there somewhere in my head. I say a silent prayer before rising from the bed, ever so slowly, careful not to wake her. She looks so peaceful. My little girl is the most precious thing in my life. I pray that she stays safe for ever. That our world is a better place for her than it was for me. And then I go downstairs, pushing my memories from my mind with varying degrees of success. I can't look at my daughter or even think of her without fearing the danger the world's predators pose. It's a curse on my life. Even now, after all this time. I'm still very much hoping the writing of this book helps loosen the evil doctor's grip.

* * *

I forced a reluctant smile when I re-joined Nicola in the lounge, hoping for a convivial evening, a film, something light-hearted, maybe a few chocolates, and a drink or two, Scotch whisky, my usual chemical cosh of choice to numb the pain. But my wife had other ideas in mind, so very different to mine, and I can't blame her for that. She turned the TV off almost as soon as I entered the room, a serious expression on her face. But at least her expression was genuine. There's no pretence in her and she has one of those faces that only ever reflect what she's thinking. I wasn't surprised at all when she announced there was something we needed to discuss.

'Sit down, Tony, we need to talk.'

My heart sank as I settled in my seat, the tell-tale signs of anxiety already evident as I felt my temperature rise. It seemed as if she was setting me up for bad news. There was an atmosphere. I thought for one horrible moment she was about to say she wanted a divorce. But, instead, Nicola told me that she was glad I was making good progress. And I'm certain she meant it. They weren't empty words. But then she added that she was taking Olivia to stay with her maternal grandmother in London for a few days.

Nicola frowned when I fetched myself a drink, a strong golden spirit with a splash of water, declining one herself. I sat down opposite her, my generous tot of whisky in one hand. That was a mistake. Alcohol was the last thing the situation needed. It's become an all-too-common support mechanism. And it didn't help one little bit. There was a hard edge to my voice when I spoke, another mistake, reflecting my disappointment rather than anger. But I don't think Nicola realised that. I should have stayed a lot calmer than I did. It's all too easy for me to come across as argumentative, aggressive even, when that's the last thing I want. I wonder what's wrong with me sometimes. I never seem to learn. I've become my own worst enemy. I deal with these situations so very badly. Nicola's a lovely woman, intelligent, sensitive, and empathetic before I push her beyond all reason. I need to remember that. I know it can't be easy living with a man like me.

'Why go to London now of all times? It's not even the school holidays.'

She looked close to tears. 'Please calm down, Tony, I'm not looking for an argument. That's the last thing I want.'

I should have listened. I should have done exactly what she asked me to. But I didn't, I was too upset for that. My eyes widened as I leant towards her. My tone was too harsh, far too confrontational, another regret. 'I'm just asking, that's all. It's a reasonable enough question. And one that deserves an answer. Surely that's not too much to ask.'

She looked away now, avoiding my accusing stare. 'Olivia's four years old, Tony; a bit of time off school won't do her any harm at all.'

I barked out my response. 'I'm not sure her teacher would agree.'

And then a revelation, Nicola had it all worked out. 'I've

talked to the head. She understands the circumstances. It's not going to be a problem.'

I felt close to panic now. It seemed there was little else I could do. But I wasn't ready to give up quite yet. If only I'd taken a more reasonable approach. 'Circumstances, what circumstances? What the hell's that supposed to mean?'

Her voice raised in pitch and tone for the first time as her tears began to flow. My fault, I think, no, definitely my fault.

'Oh, come off it, Anthony, you have to admit you're preoccupied with the book. You're focused on the past. You're not here with me even when you're in the room. And the drinking is getting out of hand. You know that yourself. You're pissed more than you're sober. You said you were going to stop. But it's getting worse, if anything. You've gone through almost half a bottle of whisky already this week.'

I was *Anthony* again, back on the naughty step. I drained my glass, relishing the malty spirit as it burned my throat. I knew she was right. 'It's been a tough few weeks. There's been a lot of work, what with the interviews and everything. But you've encouraged me. I thought that's what you wanted. You'd need a drink, too, if you had to deal with half the shit I'm encountering. I'll quit the booze once the book's done.'

Nicola shook her head slowly, her eyes pleading as she reached out to touch my knee. 'I'm not knocking you, Tony. I do appreciate the efforts you're making, honestly, I do. And you're brilliant with Olivia, always have been. But it won't do either of us any harm to have a bit of space for a few days. It may even do us both some good. I'm only going to visit my mother. It's not as if I'm leaving you. Why make such a big deal of it?'

I took a deep breath, telling myself a more conciliatory approach might elicit a better response. But deep down, I already knew I was losing the argument. Nicola had a point. I tried to sound as fair-minded as possible when I replied. But I could feel my heart beating in my throat. I didn't want them to go. The truth is, I feared they might not come back. 'Well, what about your work?'

She sighed, rolling her eyes, I think losing patience now. I can hardly blame her for that. I make so many promises I never keep. 'I'm self-employed, Anthony. I've asked Emma to cover my classes. Yoga can wait.'

I knew when I was beaten. I'd played my last card. 'How long are you going for?'

She avoided my eyes, looking at the floor. 'I haven't decided.'

One more question. I wasn't happy, I wasn't happy at all. 'Then when are you leaving? Can you at least tell me that?'

'Tomorrow morning on the ten o'clock train. The tickets are already booked.'

I'm not ashamed to admit that I felt choked as I hurried towards the kitchen, reaching for the whisky, drinking directly from the bottle, pouring the liquid down my throat. The trip was a done deal.

And then the final dagger in my back. I said I'd run my wife and child to the station, but Nicola had already arranged a taxi. I didn't ask why. I thought I might not like the answer.

You won't be surprised to hear I slept on the sofa clutching the empty whisky bottle to my chest. It seemed like the sensible thing to do.

* * *

They left about an hour ago, and so I've got the house to myself. It feels so empty, almost deserted, I feel so alone. I was tempted to open another whisky bottle after breakfast, to drink myself into welcome oblivion. But what would that achieve beyond brief escape? It seems the drink is one of the main reasons they've gone. I need to do something about that, and quickly too. I ended up pouring the entire remaining bottle down the sink. I'll probably come to regret that, but such is life. And I can always buy another bottle if needed.

I've decided to see my involuntary isolation as an opportunity to focus on my writing. I'll get the book finished as fast as possible and then worry about relationships. It's not a selfish act. You can't change others, but you can change yourself. I genuinely believe it's the best thing I can do in the interests of my family. In many ways, the future is in my hands.

8

At my second meeting with the anonymous senior female officer, she told me of an investigative interview she'd conducted with a nervous nine-year-old boy, who I'll call Robert to protect his identity. What I'm about to recount all happened *before* I met the doctor who ruined so many lives. It still surprises me to share that. I hope I can make some sense of the facts as my writing continues. But as of now, it leaves me both angry and discouraged. If I'm honest, I think the police could have done more. It seems they let me down.

The officer undertook the interview with a senior child protection social worker named Alan Garret, now sadly deceased, at one of the county's two social services video interview facilities. Robert was already in the local authority's care at the time of the interview, living with foster carers following sexual abuse by his father. That investigation was complete, and the father imprisoned, but the boy now had more to say. He'd made a further disclosure to a foster carer, who in turn contacted the boy's social worker.

The officer shared this second investigative interview transcript with me because of its direct relevance to my own experiences at Galbraith's hand. I'll recount it as it was told to me. It may not be easy to read for some. It wasn't easy to listen to, and it wasn't easy to write.

The officer told me she was fairly new to child protection work at the time, in her early twenties. She'd been doing the job for a few months at most. But she'd completed the joint investigation training course, she was committed to the work, and she had supportive and capable colleagues she could rely on. The relevant interview was particularly challenging. But she was prepared for it. It didn't go overly well, but some significant evidence was gleaned. That information became more critical as time passed. The officer still had a clear recollection of that interview even after thirty years. But she checked the paperwork, anyway, ensuring her account accurately reflects what happened that day.

* * *

The boy had been interviewed on video once before at the same social services interview suite. But the officer and social worker explained the process again, trying to put the boy at ease, or at least, as far as was possible in the circumstances. The officer told me that no child should have to go through such things, but sadly many do. It was both her and the social worker's responsibility to ensure a purpose was served. The boy deserved the best of them. She likes to think they provided it, and I have no reason to contradict her. It was something she'd done several times before, interviewing both boys and girls of different ages. But it never got easier. It always felt like the most important job in the world. And every time, she had a fear of making an error, asking a leading question, compromising evidence. As she told her story, I asked myself how investigative professionals coped with the job's many demands. No wonder some suffer burnout. I don't think I could deal with such things for however short a time. I thank them for their efforts.

The officer told me that she, Garret, and the boy sat on bean-bags stuffed with polystyrene beads, in an eggshell-blue-painted interview room, with the video camera on and the recording equipment running. She stated the time, date, location and the names of those present before engaging the boy in conversation, asking open questions directly pertinent to his allegations, encouraging him to talk. She took the lead in line with her training.

The boy talked of further sexual offences committed by his father but then of similar violations committed by another adult male who he called 'the doctor'. It was the first time the boy had mentioned this second man in a formal interview setting. Identifying the doctor became the officer's number one priority. The remainder of the interview was, therefore, focused on that end.

'Just so we're clear, Robert. You're saying you were assaulted by an adult male doctor as well as your father?'

The boy replied, 'Yes.'

The officer told me she remembered Alan Garret reassuring the boy at that point, telling him he was doing well, that nothing that had happened to him was his fault. She said something similar and then offered the boy a tissue when he started to cry. She withdrew her hand when he didn't accept it, wiping his eyes with a sleeve of his grey jumper. She asked her next question.

'When did it happen?'

The boy said it happened in the summer, but he couldn't identify the day or even the month. The officer tried to clarify the approximate date with further questions but without success. She decided to move on.

'Where did it happen?'

Robert said it happened in a white room. And that was it; the white room became a focus of police enquiries. When she asked Robert to describe the room, he said it was covered in white tiles, like a bathroom, but there weren't any windows.

Identifying the location of the room became another top priority. Find the place, find the man.

When she asked if he'd ever seen the room before, Robert said no. Neither did he know where it was. And then another question that mattered. Could he describe the building?

To the officer's frustration and disappointment, Robert said that he couldn't, he hadn't seen it. The boy was becoming increasingly agitated, appearing troubled and anxious. But the officer decided she had no option but to continue. It was one of the most challenging aspects of the job, pressing children for information so difficult to share.

When she asked how he'd got to the room, Robert said he'd been taken there by his father. He couldn't describe the building because he'd been blindfolded and taken there by car after dark. He described the journey as long and talked of his fear, but he hadn't been able to see anything.

The officer paused at that stage of our discussion, allowing me time to consider what she'd said and to comment. She confirmed that Robert was indeed being taken to Galbraith's address, as I'd suspected. He'd been taken to the white-tiled cellar accessed via the Galbraith family kitchen, the entrance hidden behind a Welsh oak dresser. But, of course, the police didn't know that at the time. They didn't know where the white room was, nor who the doctor was. If they had, my life could have been very different. Life turns on such things, one event affecting the other.

The officer went on to tell me that she'd given up on identifying the location of the room by that stage of the interview, but not the man. She asked Robert why he'd thought the man a doctor. His father had used the title. She asked if his father ever said the doctor's name. But it then became clear that the boy had been drugged. His recollection of his time in the cellar was hazy at best. But he did say he thought he might have heard his father refer to the doctor with a name starting with a G. He was far from sure. She went on to ask for a description, but the boy's answers were vague. With hindsight, some aspects of the description Robert gave matched Galbraith's appearance. But without further evidence to suggest Galbraith was their man, the police were never going to identify him as a potential suspect. Galbraith was a well-respected senior professional considered an expert in the care of children. He was a man the police went to for advice in such cases. It makes me feel sick to my stomach thinking about it. Galbraith had so many people conned.

The officer soon realised they wouldn't get any further with Robert, however many questions she asked. It was time to bring matters to a close. She did, however, ask Robert one last thing. Why hadn't he told them about the doctor at the first interview?

'I was... I was too scared. My dad was scared of the doctor and I am, too.'

'Are you saying you were more scared of the doctor than of your father, even after everything your father did to you?'

Robert curled up in a ball, pulling his knees to his chest. His entire body was trembling, but it didn't stop him talking. 'The doctor kills people, Dad told me he's a very scary man.'

'You're safe now, you do understand that, don't you?'

The boy sat up, nodded once, but said no more.

* * *

The interviewers brought the interview to a close. The officer completed the practical tasks required of her by the rules of evidence, headed downstairs to the kitchen for a hot drink, and then contacted her boss. She only had to wait for a few seconds before speaking to Trevor Simpson, then a Detective Inspector responsible for child protection services for the force. She outlined everything Robert had said succinctly and professionally before Simpson responded.

'Do you think the boy's information is reliable?'

'Yeah, yeah, I do, I think he's describing *exactly* what happened to him. The poor boy's been through so much shit, it almost beggars belief. This doctor character sounds like a seriously dangerous man.'

The inspector's instructions were clear, his tone urgent. 'Okay, listen carefully, this is what I want you to do. Talk to all the child protection managers for both the force and social services. Ask them if a white room or doctor has featured in any relevant investigations. I'll have a word with the boy's father at Swansea nick. I can't see the bastard telling us much, he won't want to be seen as a grass, not in that place. But I'll put a bit of pressure on, see what I can do. I'd happily cut the cunt's balls off with a rusty blade if it were up to me.'

Yes, the police were on Galbraith's trail. There wasn't sufficient evidence yet, far from it, but it was building. He was now the hunted, but sadly, not quickly enough for me. My first appointment with Galbraith had been fast approaching. I still wish things had been different. But, as I've said before, we can't rewrite the past. I can strive to understand what happened, maybe come to terms with it. But I can't change it.

I asked the officer what became of the enquiries ordered by DI Simpson before I left West Wales Police Headquarters for the final time. The answer made it clear the picture was building. A white room had featured in at least three investigations over the years. There was a young lad of six in August 1984 who'd mentioned being taken to a white room by an uncle; then something telling, something awful happened. The Crown Prosecution Service had dropped the case. Galbraith had provided 'therapy'.

He put the boy's terrible allegations down to nightmares. Any chance of prosecution was lost. The other two cases in 1987 and 1989 also involved boys of similar ages. The children's names were placed on the child protection register under the sexual abuse category, multi-agency child protection plans were implemented, but once again, there hadn't been sufficient evidence for prosecutions. The information related to the white room was informative, but sadly, it didn't identify the location. All the children involved lived within a five-mile radius of Galbraith's home. One, a six-year-old boy, had talked of being filmed. I first encountered Galbraith in the winter of 1992. Things could have been so very different.

Maybe, just maybe, the police really didn't have enough information to identify Galbraith as an abuser at that point. I could excuse their inaction based on that limited evidence. I hoped that my interviews with Mel Nicholson and DS Forsyth would help clarify matters and give me some peace.

9

All this talk brought back vivid memories and I couldn't help but think of my first visit to the child guidance clinic. It was a pivotal day, my first meeting with the doctor who offered nothing but misery. I've gone over that day again and again, covered it in a second interview with my mother and even pressured my father and big sister to talk about it. But my mother's memories seemed clearer than either mine or theirs. She remembers every second of that day with a burning intensity, each detail etched on her mind, I suspect, for ever. We talked in the pleasant kitchen of the same detached Welsh stone cottage where I spent my childhood.

Before the interview began, my mother made two cups of peppermint tea sweetened with a little local honey. It's been her hot drink of choice for as long as I can remember. She sipped hers as she sat opposite me at the old pine table with which I was so familiar. I could see the stress on my mother's lovely face as she shifted uneasily in her chair. She wasn't looking forward to the interview, and she'd made that perfectly clear in the unequivocal language I couldn't fail to understand. But she was committed to taking part in the interests of my wellbeing. I'm grateful to her for her selfless act of kindness. And I want to make one thing crystal clear right from the very start. My mother bears no guilt. I bear her no malice. I've never blamed her for what happened at Galbraith's hand, and I never will. I don't think she's ever entirely accepted that, but it's true. If or when this becomes a book, I hope she reads it and understands. If I can give her that one gift, I'll be a happy man.

* * *

'Are you ready to make a start, Mum?'

My mother sighed, fidgeting with her cuff. 'As ready as I'll ever be.'

I wanted to ease the interview process, to make it as painless as possible. 'An hour at most, and it'll all be over,' I coaxed.

She cleared her throat, the remnants of a winter cold still lingering. She blew her nose before speaking. 'Okay, where do I start?'

'How about at the beginning?'

She nodded once, seemingly resigned to the inevitable.

'Okay, here goes, let's get this done. I'll cast my mind back in time.'

I switched on the recording equipment. 'Thank you, please go ahead, I'm listening.'

'I thought we'd be waiting months for that first appointment, but Galbraith's letter came quickly. And I was pleased, can you believe that? The appointment was just a few days away. It was a huge relief. Be careful what you wish for.'

'You couldn't possibly have known what was to come.'

She screwed up her face. 'Things were really bad at home. Your behaviour was getting worse. You were missing your father terribly, and I wasn't coping. I thought I was doing the right thing for you, me, and all of us. If I could turn back the clock, I'd make a different decision.'

'I know, Mum, I know, you don't need to keep saying it.'

'The letter said we all had to go to that first appointment, me, you, your father and Siân. Dad was dead against the idea. He'd moved out to live with that young tart. The last thing he wanted was to spotlight his infidelity. And Siân tried everything to get out of it. But I persuaded them both for your sake. I used everything in my power to encourage them to go, and they did. I've never regretted anything as much in my life.'

All I could do was repeat myself as she began to cry. 'Galbraith had his twisted reasons for his rapid response. But you couldn't possibly have known that,' I reassured her. 'Nothing that happened was anybody's responsibility but his. You need to accept that. You've been blaming yourself for years. It's time to stop.'

My mother dabbed at her eyes with a paper tissue taken from a box on the table next to her. 'Do you really need the detail?'

'Yes, please, Mum, everything you can remember.'

She sighed. 'Okay, let's get this over with. I got up early on the morning of the appointment. I prepared breakfast and then got you and Siân up about an hour later. You watched TV until Dad arrived to collect us in that flash new car you were so very impressed with.'

I nodded, the memory still clear in my mind. 'Ah, yes, the white convertible.'

Mother grimaced. 'I hated that thing. Your father could be a selfish git at times. He wasn't as forthcoming with the maintenance money as he should have been. I so wanted to tell him what I thought of him. But I decided the appointment had to come first. Tensions were bad enough already. I remember leading you and Siân towards the car after your father sounded the horn. I don't think he could face coming into the cottage. And then he kept trying to get the three of us chatting during the journey. About ordinary things, nothing to do with the clinic. He was trying to make us laugh. It was just so inappropriate. As if nothing out of the ordinary was happening. As if he'd never left. That's the way he was. He's a different man now, thank God. He's matured. Things have changed. But back then, I could have slapped him and slapped him hard. Coping with him took the patience of a saint.'

I drained my cup, relishing the sweet honey at the bottom. And then a question that took us to the crux of the story.

'What happened when we arrived at the clinic?'

She pressed her lips together, fingering her bead necklace as she spoke. 'Your father parked the car, I told the three of you to get out, and then I led you all into reception. That nice receptionist welcomed us. Do you remember her? It was a long time ago, but I can still picture her now, standing there.'

I gave a wry smile. 'Her name's Sharon Breen. I spoke to her only recently, as it happens, at her home, a council house on the edge of town. She's a *very* different person now. Not nearly as friendly as you remember her. I don't think you'd like her quite as much these days.'

Mother continued, choosing to ignore my observations. 'Galbraith kept us waiting in reception for about fifteen minutes. I remember Sharon apologising, saying he wouldn't be too long, that he must be doing something important.'

'I've got my theories on that.'

Mother's face took on a puzzled expression. 'Such as?'

'I think it was all part of his game, leaving us sitting there, showing us who was boss.'

'You may well be right.'

'Oh, I'm certain of it.'

Mother linked her fingers together as if in prayer. 'Do you remember when he did finally make an appearance?'

I nodded. 'Yeah, yeah, I do. Galbraith stood there in the doorway, dressed in a grey suit, a white shirt, and a brightly coloured tie covered in cartoon characters. The tie grabbed my attention, as I'm sure it was intended to. And there were shiny silver buckles on his shoes. You couldn't miss those either. He wasn't like any doctor I'd seen before. All part of the act. All part of a character he created to con and control.'

My mother nodded her agreement before responding. 'He was a good-looking man, and there's no denying that. I can see him now as if it were yesterday: his short black hair, piercing blue eyes, and those ridiculously white teeth. He was a person who liked to make a big impression. That was obvious from the start.'

'He shook each of our hands in turn.'

Mother sipped her tea before setting her cup back on its matching saucer. A second or two passed before she spoke. 'Yes, he did, starting with me; I think of that as deliberate. He identified me as the matriarch and used it against me.'

'Do you remember what he said?'

She threw both her hands out wide, more expansive than I'd seen her in some considerable time. Her impromptu impression was surprisingly effective. 'Welcome, welcome, marvellous to see you all. Please accept my sincere apologies for keeping you waiting. Unavoidable, I'm afraid, something of an emergency. I'm certain Sharon here has been looking after you. Please join me in my office. I'm sure we'll all have an extremely productive morning.'

'Yeah, that's right, it was something along those lines. The bastard was directing events right from the very start. He knew exactly what he was doing. We never stood a chance.'

Mother raised a hand to her throat, her eyes focused on me.

'Galbraith moved to the centre of the room and told us to sit in chairs placed in a semicircle so that each of us was facing him. His chair was bigger and higher than ours. He'd thought of everything.'

'All part of his plan.'

'I remember sitting to Galbraith's left with you next to me. Dad sat to his right with Siân next to him. I was feeling increasingly nervous by that stage. The situation was so alien to my experience. So far outside my comfort zone. I suspect we all felt the same. The bastard was pulling the strings. He had us *exactly* where he wanted us,' my mother said before continuing. 'Galbraith pointed to a camera high in one corner of the room and microphones on each of the walls. He told us he recorded therapy sessions, claiming it was an essential part of the process. He kept using that word, therapy, therapy, *fucking* therapy! It makes me so damned angry. It was all about the therapy. And then he asked if I had any objections to the use of the camera. What could I say? I thought he was going to help you. I felt I had to cooperate.'

I don't think I'd ever heard my mother swear before, never once in my life. It sounded somehow wrong coming from her mouth. It's strange how we put people in boxes.

'He was playing you, Mum. Just like he did everyone else.'

'I felt I had to agree, and I nodded. I couldn't find the words. My confidence was slipping. And then Galbraith made us move seats, you next to him. You started crying when he touched your arm. You tried to move back closer to me, but I told you to do as the doctor said. I so regret that. What was I thinking? I gave him the power. He was in control.'

I felt genuine sympathy for my mother. I could see her angst, her shrinking body language as her shoulders curled over her chest, the mournful expression on her face.

'It was a more naïve time, Mum. People trusted authority figures. You were trying to do your best for me, no more than that.'

Mother reached out to squeeze my hand. 'Thanks, cariad.'

That word brought back memories. Cariad means love in Welsh and it was the name my mother called me from time to time when I was small. She used it less now, but I've never doubted her love.

I asked my next question, keen to move the interview along. 'What happened next?'

My mother let out a groan. 'It was bizarre. It would be funny if it weren't so serious. Galbraith reached behind him, opened a desk drawer, and took out a bag of lemon sherbets. He offered you a sweet and then took one himself, unwrapping it slowly and popping it into his mouth when you didn't take one. It was like a theatrical display, everything exaggerated. He kept saying how delicious it was. And then he encouraged you to take one for a second time.'

'And I did.'

'We all did. Can you believe that? We all sat there in the bastard's office sucking sweets. I thought it was ridiculous at first, but then you grinned, you started to relax. And I did too. I began to think I could trust this doctor with his unusual methods. I even started to like him. That makes me sick to my stomach when I think of it now.'

'He wanted you to like him. It was a performance. It was a routine he'd followed many times before. He was directing events with skill and aplomb. It's what the bastard did, it's how he operated.'

'I know, Tony. One minute we were eating sweets, and then, all of a sudden, he got serious. He kept stressing the urgency of the situation, saying you needed his help. He made us all talk about our family break-up, how it had affected each of us and the effects on you. Dad and Siân didn't say very much at all, they just wanted out of there, but I did my best because I thought that was the right thing to do. It wasn't easy talking about everything that had happened. But I was trying to help you. Galbraith said he needed that information to inform your treatment plan.'

'And then he announced he'd need to see me alone.'

My mother's face paled. She looked suddenly older. As if the memory had temporarily aged her. 'I stiffened when he said that. I should have listened to my gut. But Galbraith was persuasive. He had an answer for everything.'

'He was a skilled manipulator, influencing us all with his unscrupulous ways.'

'You put it so much better than I could, Tony.'

I knew she was flattering me, boosting my mood because she could, making me feel better about myself. But I went along with it. The metaphorical pat on the back felt good. 'It's the journalist in me, all part of the job.'

Her resulting smile disappeared as quickly as it appeared. 'Do you remember the typed agreement Galbraith made us all sign? I've still got a copy somewhere. I should have burned the damned thing years ago.'

'I've got a vague recollection but no more than that.'

She rubbed the back of her neck, massaging it with her hand. 'It said you had to complete the entire course of treatment and introduced the possibility of him seeing you at his home. When I asked for an explanation, he said he sometimes saw patients there when they needed more intensive therapy than the clinic's busy schedule allowed. Looking back, it should have sounded alarm bells. I still feel so guilty about that. But at least I asked. Your father didn't say anything at all. He just sat there waiting for it all to be over.'

'You've got *nothing* to feel guilty about, Mum, and there's nothing to forgive.'

'I think Galbraith had achieved everything he wanted from the appointment by then. He showed us the therapy room to bring things to a close.'

'Bright yellow paint, cartoon murals, a bit like his tie, navy-blue beanbags, a TV, video recorder and a wall-mounted camera.'

She began slowly rocking in her seat, back and forth in rhythmic movement, first one way and then the other. 'And a red light above the door. He was so very keen to bring that to our attention. No entry under any circumstances if it was on. He repeated it twice as if we hadn't heard him the first time. What a total and utter bastard that man really was.'

I closed my eyes. It was as if I was back there, picturing the scene. I could see the room, the colours, the textures, Galbraith's leering face, looking me up and down. 'He had a framed photo of his wife and daughters on his desk and a poster covering the window in his office door. The perfect family man, someone you could trust.'

'Galbraith was so very keen to arrange the next appointment, to see both of us initially, and then you alone. He told Dad and Siân they didn't need to come. I remember how impatient he was when Sharon couldn't find an early enough date in the diary for his liking. He seemed so disappointed that the next available time was two weeks away.'

'Oh, he was disappointed all right. I bet the perverted bastard couldn't wait to see me again.'

Mum dropped her head. 'I took his eagerness as a sign of his desire to help you. He was a doctor. He had a good reputation. The GP had said as much. Why wouldn't I think that way?'

I touched her right arm just above the elbow. 'I'm sure I'd have done the same in your place.'

'Really, would you, really?'

'Galbraith conned an awful lot of people for a very long time. You were no different to anyone else.'

She blew out a long slow breath and stood, leaving the room for a few minutes for a bathroom visit. I could see she'd been crying when she finally returned to the kitchen. She looked back, meeting my eyes as she approached the kettle on a worktop close to a double-glazed window with its view of the garden. She was trying to put on a brave face. And I knew it was for my sake as much as her own.

'Another cuppa?'

'I'll have a black coffee with a drop of whisky if you've got it. Irish, Scotch or American, anything will do.'

She shuddered slightly as she handed me my hot drink, strong, black, but alcohol-free. 'I'm absolutely exhausted, Tony. Do you mind if we talk about the second appointment another time? That's enough for today.'

I checked my online diary. Revisiting the past is never easy. I was weary too. Maybe it was time for a break. And I needed that drink. The nearest pub was calling.

'How about next Tuesday morning at ten?'

Her relief was almost palpable. 'Okay, cariad, it will give me a few days to think. Let's talk then.'

10

To date, my interview with Gary Davies was my most unpleasant and challenging by far. Even my meeting with Sharon Breen, with all her misguided antagonism, paled by comparison. I didn't like Davies; I can't pretend otherwise. It was as much as I could do to stop myself from punching his lights out. It would have felt so very good to ram his nicotine-stained teeth down his ugly throat. I've never loathed a man more. But such physical aggression will remain a fantasy, more's the pity. I'm not sure if I'm capable of such things. But I guess none of us truly knows until the situation demands.

Davies hadn't been on my list of interviewees, but he reached out to me after he saw a social media post I'd made about writing the book. The powers that be at the prison saw his contacting me as contributing to his rehabilitative process. It seems confession is good for the soul.

Davies has a long history of sexual offences. He's been in and out of prison for years, offending, remorse, fantasy, and offending, repeating the same predictable pattern. He's currently serving an eighteen-month custodial sentence for the indecent assault of an eight-year-old girl. His message contained all that information and more. None of which interested me in itself.

There's any number of predators out there. He's one of many. But the final paragraph of his communication got my attention: thirty years ago, he and Galbraith were members of the same organised abuse ring.

That was it. I knew I had to talk to him. As despicable as Davies most certainly is, he's a valuable source of information. I had to tap into him. I didn't have a choice.

I felt strangely conflicted as I drove towards HM Prison Swansea in the Sandfields area of the sprawling Welsh seaside city. I didn't want to spend time with the man, but I was desperate to interview him. He'd have information to share, things to tell me. Maybe something that no one else knew.

* * *

Davies was seated and waiting with his arms crossed when I entered an allocated room in the large Victorian stone building. He stood to shake hands, but the accompanying guard, a well-muscled man with a shaved head and military tattoos on both forearms, ordered him to sit, for which I was grateful. I didn't want to touch his hand. Just being in his presence made me feel dirty. But I was there for a reason. I struggled to retain a professional persona. It wasn't easy, but I somehow managed it. The guard sat behind Davies, watching and listening without saying a word.

Davies spoke for almost half an hour without the need for encouragement. It poured out of him like a caustic flood. He was keen to talk about his time as a member of the paedophile ring, repeatedly expressing feelings of regret that were far from persuasive. I noted he became increasingly animated as he described the various offences he witnessed, always minimising his culpability. He went into far more detail than was necessary, taking obvious pleasure in the telling. He insisted he was a changed man. But I'm sure that couldn't be further from the truth. I noticed a prominent bulge in his grey tracksuit trousers as he described one particularly violent rape committed by Galbraith. Davies was drooling, sweating, red in the face. I asked him if his words were a confession of sorts, but he was quick to deny it, insisting that Galbraith was wholly responsible. I could have argued the point, but I saw no purpose. Davies had mentioned the doctor. It seemed an ideal opportunity to ask more.

Davies had a knowing smirk on his face as he talked of the doctor. He referred to Galbraith with obvious reverence. He was a man Davies looked up to. That couldn't have been clearer. 'Dr Galbraith once told me he could spot and target a vulnerable child within seconds on first sight. It was a skill he used many times to his great advantage. Fucking brilliant! The man was a star. Not that I'd do that, of course, not now I'm being rehabilitated.'

I couldn't hold back my anger even in the interests of the interview. Davies's words got to me, they stung. He was so full of shit. 'What you've told me doesn't surprise me in the slightest. It's the sort of man Galbraith was, a bizarre creature, a moral vacuum. And you're not much better, and that's if you're better at all. Men like you don't change. You are what you are. You do what you do, always a risk, always a menace.'

He didn't look in the least bit fazed. I suspect he'd heard it all before, and worse, a lot worse. If anything, he found my words amusing. I became increasingly convinced he was having a good time. And that rehabilitation crap, it was bullshit, no more than that.

'I'm serving my time. I'm having counselling. You've asked your fucking questions and I've told you what I know. It's not my fault you don't like the answers. What more do you want? I'm a model prisoner. It won't be long till I'm out of here.'

I looked Davies directly in the eye, refusing to blink, refusing to look away. I didn't want him to identify any weaknesses. I wanted to scream out a string of heartfelt insults, but instead I swallowed my words before focusing back on the interview. That's why I was there, after all. I needed to stay in control. 'Tell me about the abuse ring. Did the doctor play a significant role?'

Davies laughed a hoarse tobacco-ravaged laugh that reverberated around the room. 'Significant? Give me a fucking break. Galbraith was the leader, the main man! All the others were shit scared of him, not just the kids but the adults, too. He was one vicious bastard. He even shocked me sometimes. He used to kill animals in front of the kids, kittens, puppies, you know, to shut the little fuckers up.'

I felt my chest tighten as he continued talking.

'Galbraith used to call our group Pet Club, his little joke. We met in farm buildings, loads of us, some local, some not, like-minded men, and lots of kids of all ages from different families. There must have been at least a hundred of the little sods all told at one time or another while I was involved. It had been going on for years. Some of us met in prison, others in therapy groups, friends of friends. Some of the abusers, if that's what you want to call them, had even been members of the club as kids themselves. You'd be amazed how many of us there are out there. Men who like their sexual interests on the younger side. And Galbraith was in charge. He was our leader. We all thought he was a fucking hero. He could shut a kid up, no problem at all.'

I fought to regain my composure. Davies wanted a reaction. I didn't give him the satisfaction. I'd never hated a man more. 'Did Galbraith ever involve his daughters?'

'Nah, he had no interest in girls.'

'What about patients?'

'Yeah, of course, young boys who'd keep their stupid mouths shut, when he knew he could get away with it. He knew which ones to target, which ones to leave alone. The man was a fucking genius.'

I'd heard enough by that stage. There was only so much I could take. Davies wasn't an easy man to listen to. Galbraith was a devil. And Davies was cut from the same demonic cloth. I stood to leave, but Davies called me back. And then he told me things that genuinely shook me to the core. He kept me there for another fifteen minutes after that, talking at me, not to me. It poured out of him with no hesitation, one sentence blurring into another. He took apparent pleasure in the telling, revelling in my discomfort. I feared my legs might give way as the room became an impressionist blur. I dry gagged once, then again. If it weren't for the guard grabbing my arm at the opportune time, I'd have hit the floor hard.

* * *

I headed for the nearest Swansea off-licence as soon as I got out of there. Sobriety could wait for another day. Tonight, would be a time for drinking. Oblivion beckoned and it couldn't come quickly enough. Another hangover was a price worth paying.

I hate the idea of Davies being released. It eats away at me, beats me down. They have him now, but they'll let him out again, he'll even likely get time off for good behaviour if he shows remorse. Men like Davies usually serve half their sentence if they play the game, that's the norm. Not many people realise that. I only learnt it recently myself. He'll be back on the streets some-time soon. It could be weeks, or even days. He's conned the authorities, just as Galbraith did. For a time, I chose to forget.

11

I decided to take a short break from writing after finishing my most recent chapter to visit my wife and daughter in London. Nicola wasn't responding to my calls or texts. I tried her mother's landline, but there was no reply on that either. She's got one of those landlines that display the caller's number. I had a horrible feeling there was a female conspiracy to ignore me. It was a toss-up between getting drunk again or buying a train ticket. I eventually decided on the ticket – a more difficult choice than it should have been.

I struggled with being alone in the house, particularly after my visit to Swansea Prison. Alcohol takes the edge off, it blunts the edges, but it solves nothing. The truth is the situation was really getting to me. If Nicola wants out of our marriage, I'd rather she say something. Dealing with the baggage of the past is bad enough without dealing with relationship uncertainties too. I still love the woman dearly, and Olivia, too. I'm fearful of losing them. There's only so much any man can bear.

I caught an early-morning train from west Wales to Paddington, then a taxi to Victoria, and another overland train from there. I originally planned to walk to my mother-in-law's house from Blackheath Station after a quick cup of coffee in the café opposite, but I changed my mind, calling an Uber. It had started raining, the sky overcast, and so it made sense to stay dry. The journey took no longer than ten minutes and would have been quicker still if it wasn't for the volume of the London traffic. That always surprises me, however many times I visit the city. The contrast with west Wales is dramatic in that and so many other respects. I'm not saying I dislike London. I like to visit. There's an energy about the place I find stimulating. But Wales calls me back. I like arriving home even more.

I had an uneasy feeling deep in the pit of my stomach as I walked up the concrete path towards my mother-in-law's black-painted front door with its polished brass furniture. I knocked, reticently at first, and then harder with the knuckles of my right hand, resigned to facing whatever the future held. The look on my mother-in-law's face when she opened the door didn't help.

'Tony, I wasn't expecting you. Are you sober? You look exhausted.'

Not exactly the welcome I'd hoped for, but it could have been worse. If I had been drunk, it wouldn't have been the first time. The question wasn't as unreasonable as it seemed.

'Yeah, yeah, I am, not a drop has passed my lips. Good to see you, too. Can I come in?'

Helen, that's my mother-in-law's name, Helen Lee, stepped aside when my daughter entered the hall behind her, running towards me with a loving smile that raised my flagging spirits. I lifted Olivia up from the tiled floor, holding her close, not wanting to let her go. But then she said, 'Mummy's in bed,' which for some reason concerned me more than I can explain. It was a matter of instinct. Something told me that something was very wrong. As it happened, things weren't as bad as I feared.

Olivia led me into her grandmother's spacious, expensively furnished lounge, where several plastic dolls and a collection of their multi-coloured clothing were scattered on the cream wool carpeted floor. Olivia picked up a favourite doll, handing it to me as Helen stood behind her, her expression darkening with each second that passed. Helen put one of Olivia's favourite cartoons on the television, handed her a packet of jelly beans, encouraged her to watch the programme with feigned enthusiasm, and then led me to the spacious kitchen, where she sat me down at the breakfast bar. I could tell Helen had something to say to me but was reluctant to say it. It's not like her to be so reticent. Maybe she couldn't find the words.

'What is it, Helen? Is Nicola leaving me? I know something's going on.'

She gripped one hand with the other. 'Why would you ask me that?'

'I've seen it coming for weeks.'

She pulled her head back. 'That's not what's happening here.'

'Then what the hell is it? Is she ill?'

Helen swallowed hard. I could see from her expression that she wasn't finding our conversation any easier than I was.

'Nicola has told me all about everything that's happening, Tony. She's proud of what you're doing. She wants the book written as much as you do. She fully appreciates that it's something you've got to do. But she's tired, and she's struggling, she needs a break, a bit of me-time. You're drinking too much, you must realise that. And it's changed you, you're not the man you were, the man she could rely on. You need to deal with it and give her some space. That's the best thing you can do for her right now. She still loves you. That hasn't changed. Finish the book, sort yourself out, get sober, deal with your demons, and things will get better with time.'

I rushed my reply; I suspect sounding more agitated than the situation warranted. Thinking about it now, I know she was well-meaning, there was no malice in her words. But I find it difficult to trust sometimes, no doubt a legacy of my past. I asked the obvious question. 'You say she still loves me. Then why hasn't she answered my calls?'

'She's lost her phone.'

I almost believed it. 'I need to hear it from her.'

Helen sighed, I suspect disappointed with my response. 'Nicola had a headache; she's taken one of my sleeping tablets, let her sleep. The poor girl is emotionally exhausted. All the stress at home, well, it's just been too much. You need to let her rest. I genuinely think she may have a breakdown if things carry on as they are.'

I hate to admit that in that moment, all I could think about was myself. Not an easy thing to face up to, but it's true. I really am a loathsome creature at times. 'Can I stay the night?' It felt like an age before my mother-in-law answered, but it was, in reality, a matter of seconds.

'Just the *one* night. Talk to Nicola in the morning and then go back to Wales. Stop drinking, finish your book, and she'll join you when she's ready. I like you, Tony. It's good advice. You need to take it on board.'

I felt inclined to argue, but deep down, I knew Helen was right. I tend to self-destruct when under any kind of pressure I can't control. I was determined not to make this one of those times. I was desperate for a drink, never more so in my life, but I resisted that temptation too.

I spent the evening playing various childhood games with Olivia, hide and seek, make-believe, mums and dads, dolls, doing the things little girls like to do. And then I went to bed early, where I read *Siena*, a complex, enjoyable thriller by fellow

Welsh writer Phil Rowlands, until I fell asleep a little after eleven.

* * *

I was already in the kitchen, enjoying a bowl of cereal with Olivia, when Nicola finally made an appearance at around eight-thirty the following morning. Nicola smiled, stretched and yawned when she saw me. Either Helen had told her of my unexpected arrival, or Nicola hid her surprise well. I was both relieved and delighted when she leaned in to kiss my stubbled face, her full lips lingering for a few seconds before she pulled away. I hadn't expected that. That one act of physical affection meant so very much. In my eyes, it said a thousand words.

Helen looked after Olivia after breakfast, allowing me and Nicola to walk together across the heath, through Greenwich Park with its views of St Paul's Cathedral and beyond, and towards the river. We enjoyed a cup of strong coffee and a shared slice of banana cake in a pleasant café and talked, with openness and honesty, something we hadn't done for a very long time. I'm not saying it was an easy conversation, but it was meaningful.

Nicola sat opposite me, squeezed my hand and smiled without parting her lips. There was a familiar glint in her lovely eyes, but an unmistakable wariness too that no amount of make-up could possibly hide.

'I *have* lost my phone. What Mum told you was true. She didn't make it up.'

'I believe you, millions wouldn't.'

She laughed at my predictably cliched comment and then became more serious, a frown replacing her smile.

'How's the book going, are you still making progress?'

I wondered how much to say. I could have talked for hours.

But instead, I told her of the facts which seemed most important to me. Or at least those I could face verbalising when sober.

'Yeah, it's, er, it's going okay. There's been some surprises, things I hadn't expected.'

She slurped her coffee, wiping her mouth with her hand. 'Such as?'

'The police already had evidence of a white room and an abusive doctor by the time of my first clinic appointment.'

Nicola clutched my hand again, squeezing it more tightly this time. 'Oh God, I'm so sorry, Tony, that's awful. Why on earth didn't they arrest Galbraith before, well, you know what I mean, before you met him?'

'That's, er, that's one of the things I'm trying to find out.'

'I think you're incredibly brave doing what you're doing, facing the past head on. And I'm sure it's going to be a powerful book when you're finished.'

'Thanks, I, er, I appreciate your support.'

She smiled again but didn't say anything. I was ready to focus back on us, ready to change the subject. I released my hand from hers, looking her in the eye.

'Look, Nicola, I have to ask. Why on earth did you go to the station by taxi when I offered to give you a lift? I just don't understand why you'd do that. I know we'd argued, but come on, it was a little dramatic, don't you think?'

'It's not a big deal, Tony. Please don't read anything into it. I thought you were under enough pressure without having to run me and Olivia around. I thought I was being helpful giving you the time and space to get on with other things. Every little helps.'

She'd spoken with passion, as if she meant every single word, as if it was all the truth and nothing but the truth. I decided not to challenge her, to accept it at face value despite my lingering doubts. It was easier that way. And I so wanted to believe everything between us would be okay.

'I'm sorry, I'll try to be more trusting in future. I want to be a better man for you, a better husband, a better father. And I'll address the drinking, I promise I will. I give you my word. I can only apologise for how bad things have been. I'll do whatever it takes.'

She stood to hug me before returning to her seat to finish her coffee. And then we talked about other things, ordinary things unrelated to the past. It felt good to be in her company again. There was still a tension but a warmth, too. I hoped she still loved me as I loved her.

We held hands as we strolled back towards the house. I had new strength, a renewed confidence in our relationship, as if our issues, while still existing, had taken on a different, less challenging perspective. And I hope Nicola felt it too. We hugged again before entering the house, where we spent quality time with Olivia until it was time for me to leave to catch my train that afternoon.

I don't know if I read too much into it, but there was something about Nicola's countenance as she waved me off that suggested a part of her was relieved to see me go. My observation may or may not be accurate. I'm not always a good judge of such things.

I shrugged off my dark mood as I journeyed back to Wales, focusing on how good I'd felt as Nicola and I walked back to Helen's house. It was time to continue writing, time to get back to my book.

I did some basic editing on the four-hour train journey, making productive use of the time rather than just sit there watching the world pass by. And then I continued from there, the words flowing with surprising speed, the chapters appearing quickly on the page.

I've cast my mind back to my troubled childhood. And I'm making reasonably good progress. I'm determined to keep going, one often traumatic page at a time, until I reach the end. My interview with Mel Nicholson comes next. A meeting that was both informative and enlightening, and one that shocked me to the core. It's a more complex tale than I ever imagined. So many others were affected by the events surrounding my childhood. It wasn't just me.

12

I interviewed Mel Nicholson at his home, an impressive detached red-brick house in a quiet tree-lined street with a large well-tended garden, only a ten-minute drive from where I live, although my property is significantly more modest than his. I was met at the front door by an attractive middle-aged ginger-haired woman with pale blue eyes and subtle make-up, who introduced herself as Nicholson's wife.

I sat in a comfortably furnished lounge, drinking a welcome cup of strong percolated coffee, waiting for a few brief minutes until the former child protection social work manager returned from walking the dog on the nearby estuary beach. Nicholson made his apologies when he joined me and then went on to tell me he'd been surprised to receive my call. By a strange coincidence, Nicholson, a slim, clean-shaven man in his early sixties with thinning grey hair and black plastic-framed glasses, is now an author himself, not that that's of any particular relevance to my story. It did give us a common interest in addition to our strangely linked history. I think that may well have helped oil the conversational wheels.

I liked Nicholson almost as soon as I met him. He was happy to talk to me, pleased to help, with no hidden agenda or apparent prejudices that I could identify. He told me that he'd taken early retirement at a relatively young age on the grounds of ill health. Something he put down to the stress of the job. A burnout he'd recognised in others, both child protection social workers and police officers alike, but not in himself. He was in a better place by the time I met him. Social work now felt like a different life.

I asked Nicholson if he'd known Galbraith. He told me that he had. Galbraith, he said, was known to all those in child protection. The doctor was a prominent character with a big personality, who'd worked with many of the children known to the social services department, the most vulnerable in society. It was a massive surprise to Nicholson when the truth of the doctor's heinous offending became known. He'd thought he'd seen it all, that he could no longer be shocked even by the worst of crimes, but he'd been wrong. He still thought of Galbraith as the most wicked and dangerous abuser he'd ever had the misfortune to encounter. I nodded my acknowledgement. It was an opinion with which it was impossible to argue. When I took out my notepad and asked my questions, I was genuinely interested to hear the answers.

'Did you ever have even the *slightest* suspicion that Galbraith was an offender? Even a hint?'

Nicholson shook his head. 'No, *no way*, not in the slightest! Not for a single second. I didn't particularly like the man. He was always so very full of himself, but then a lot of doctors are. You know, that condescending, superior air some of them display? But a predatory sex offender, no way. It never crossed my mind. The man had me completely conned. No one was more surprised than me.'

Nicholson's answer didn't surprise me. It was confirmation

rather than revelation. I'd already established Galbraith was a skilled manipulator. He even deceived the experts. Nicholson was far from alone in that regard.

'Okay, thank you, that's very clear. Let's move on. When did you first become aware of the organised abuse ring?'

Nicholson repeatedly tapped a leg with the first two fingers of his right hand as he spoke. 'It all came completely out of the blue. I was in the office kitchen one morning making coffee when my admin officer shouted down the corridor. Karen Smith, one of my child care team managers, was on the phone. She'd said the call was urgent. I trusted her judgement. If Karen said it was urgent, it was.'

Nicholson had my attention. I *needed* to learn more. 'What did she tell you?'

'There was a brief silence before she spoke, and when she did, I could hear the tension in her voice. She was usually so composed, so self-confident, but not this time. There was none of her usual jokey humour. She was stuttering, repeating herself. And then she just blurted it out. We had a paedophile ring operating in our area. That was one hell of a thing to hear. My first instinct was to hope she was wrong. But I knew that was unlikely. She made very few mistakes. And she wasn't a woman prone to overreaction or exaggeration. She was a straight talker, no bullshit. She'd been doing the job for a long time, and she was good at it – one of the best.'

I moved to the edge of my seat, keen for Nicholson to expand on what he'd already said. 'What else did she say?'

'It wasn't good. Karen's team had been working with a family of three children, two girls of eight and six and a boy of four. All three were in foster care following the alleged rape of the eight-year-old girl by the father. The mother was siding with the abuser despite expert medical evidence corroborating the girl's allegations. She had bruising to her shoulders, back and buttocks, adult grip marks on her upper arms, internal injuries that could only have been caused in one way. It didn't take a genius to work out the allegations were true. The father was remanded in custody in Swansea Prison pending Crown Court trial.'

I could feel my heart rate increasing. There were sweat patches under both my arms. 'That's one of the worst things I've ever heard, but where does the organised abuse ring fit in?'

'Yes, I was just coming to that. As I said, the three children were placed with foster parents, a dedicated, experienced couple who'd been fostering for years. Once the children felt safe enough to talk, they all had things to say. When they started talking, they *really* started talking. All three described being taken on several occasions to a barn-like building in the back of a lorry along with other children of varying ages. While there, they were sexually assaulted by multiple offenders, relations, family friends, acquaintances and strangers – all adults, mostly men, and a small number of women, who appeared to be acting under the men's influence. We had no idea where the barn was or how often the ring met. The children named ten abusive adults and seventeen child victims from different families. And there were *many* more children they couldn't identify, anything up to *fifty!*'

I jerked my head back. I thought I might have misheard. 'Did you say *fifty?*'

'Yes, I'm afraid I did, and as it happens, even that was an underestimate. As it turned out, the final figure was closer to a hundred. It was terrible, Tony. I asked Karen if any of those named were known to us. And they were. She'd been going through the files. Some of the families involved had a *long* history with the department – a lot of things made sense in light of what we'd learnt. I sometimes ask myself how we missed the links for so long. I guess we weren't looking, that's the truth of it. We never thought such a thing would go on, not to that extent, not in our part of the world. And not for so long, not for generations. God knows how it started. I suspect with one family and then growing from there as others got involved over time. It was the sort of thing that happened to other people, not us. And it's a big rural area, massive, the biggest in the UK. The department covered three counties back then, most of it countryside. It wasn't difficult for the offenders to keep things hidden. Looking back, maybe Karen should have contacted me a lot sooner than she did. But when she did, I knew I had to step up. It was going to be the most challenging time of my career. There was so very much at stake.'

I felt genuine sympathy for Nicholson as he shared his story. I could see the burden history placed on his shoulders. I feel sure he saw that in me too. We had a common bond born of adversity. And it was clear from what he'd told me that many others do too.

Even after all the passing years, I could tell that Nicholson still found the details of the case as shocking as I did. Survivors suffer, but so do those tasked with protecting the innocent. That isn't something I'd considered adequately before that day. Nicholson talked with emotion. The hurt was still there. It was evident from his body language, painted on his face.

* * *

I took a deep breath, sucking in the air, composing myself, pondering Nicholson's statement. I asked him when Karen had contacted him, the specific date. When he asked me if it really mattered, I told him that it did. It mattered to me. He left the room, returning a few minutes later with an old green desk diary from the relevant time, a record he'd chosen to keep. The ex-child protection manager had considered writing a memoir himself and thought it might come in useful. My suspicions were sadly

correct. Karen Smith made that call *before* my second appointment at the child guidance clinic. That was bad enough. So difficult to accept. But what came next was worse. As Nicholson
continued talking of that time, my world became a darker place.
There was so much that the authorities knew, so much that could
have saved me.

'I was only in my late twenties. Just a kid, really, a boy with a
beard, trying to look older than I was. I'd recently returned to
Wales after a couple of years working for the NSPCC in the West
Country. It seems insane now when I look back on it, all that
responsibility at such a young age. I don't know how the hell I
coped. But I didn't think like that back then. I just got on with it.
And as bad as what Karen had told me was, there was worse to
come.'

'Worse?'

'Oh, yes, things got worse, all right. It was one revelation
after another, and none of them good. Karen asked me if I
knew Dr David Galbraith, the consultant child psychiatrist. I
told her that I did, of course I did, it went with the job. I
thought she might want me to talk to Galbraith on her behalf
to request appropriate therapy for the child victims before any
court proceedings. But that couldn't have been further from the
truth. The older two of the three children had named Galbraith
on video. They'd given accurate descriptions. They talked of
witnessing him committing numerous sexual offences against
multiple children, all preadolescent boys of similar ages. We're
talking indecent assault, gross indecency, rape, the worst kind
of crimes. There was no doubt that Galbraith, a man I'd
trusted, a man who had unsupervised, one-to-one professional
access to the most endangered children in the county, was an
active part of the ring. Not just an active part but a prolific
offender. And he was one sadistic bastard by the sound of

things. I think the worst I ever encountered. The implications were horrendous.'

I sat there trying to cope with each new revelation as Nicholson spoke with such passion and obvious angst. Many of the events he described in such a fluent and persuasive manner had happened *before* I encountered Galbraith myself. Galbraith was named as an abuser. He'd committed many truly awful crimes. Surely the police had enough to arrest the bastard before he got his evil clutches on me. My mind raced, one question after another, trying to undo the past. *Why the hell didn't they stop him?* I felt my face flush, my temperature rise, my muscles tense. I know my tone betrayed my low mood. It was more disappointment than anger, but there was anger too. An irritation I was finding it difficult to suppress. I found myself panting slightly as I spoke, sucking in the air, blowing it out in rapid bursts.

'Well, if you knew all that, if the two children named Galbraith, if you had the evidence, why wasn't something done? Children were at risk. *I was at risk!* Why didn't you do something, for fuck's sake? You said it was urgent, so why wait?'

Nicholson's eyes narrowed. He barked out his reply, a vein at his temple pulsing as he craned his neck toward me, making his case. 'Do you think we didn't want to get the bastard off the streets, locked up in a cell to rot? Of course we did! I've never wanted anything more. It ate away at me. But we had to plan. The timing of any protective action had to be right. That was the hardest decision I've ever been a part of; it kept me awake at night. And I know all the other professionals involved felt the same way. Galbraith was dangerous, a violent active abuser who was damaging so many young lives in the worst possible way. It was such a terrible betrayal of trust, an abomination. Living with that knowledge before arrests were made was absolutely horrendous. The worst time of my life by far. I can't stress that enough.'

'Then why the fuck didn't you do something to stop him? Why wait at all?'

Nicholson lowered his head, breathing deeply, his chest slowly rising and falling as he sucked in the air. 'It wasn't that simple, Tony. I wish it had been, but it wasn't. There was a process to follow, agreed multi-agency procedures. I'd written the damned things myself, so I could hardly complain. There'd been some horrendous failures in complex cases in other parts of the country, Cleveland, the Orkneys, major cases that went horribly wrong. We couldn't let our case become another failure. Many of the children involved in the ring hadn't been identified, let alone interviewed. And at that early stage, the evidence against some of the key suspects was limited at best. We needed corroboration. I can clearly recall Detective Inspector Trevor Simpson saying there was no point in arresting suspects and then letting them go again for lack of sufficient evidence. That wouldn't help anyone, the victims least of all. And we had to coordinate arrests. They couldn't be made one by one. If we'd done it that way, other offenders would have been warned. Potential evidence would have been destroyed, and children would have been beaten or threatened into silence. Some offenders may even have done a disappearing act to avoid arrest and punishment. We had to hold off any coordinated action until the evidence was there. That was the only way it was going to work.'

What Nicholson said didn't make me feel a great deal better. It didn't alleviate my feelings of deep anxiety and disappointment to any significant extent. I still despaired for those children at risk, the victims of the paedophile ring's vile attentions, and for the boy I was too. But for the first time, I did at least begin to understand the predicaments faced by the investigative agencies. Things are rarely as simple as they seem at face value. I was shaken by all that the ex-social work manager told me that day, but I needed to know more for my book and for the sake of my sanity too. I'd started the journey and knew I had to finish it.

Every part of my being was crying out for a drink, any form of alcohol to settle my nerves, and the stronger, the better. But I cast my fragile emotions aside as best I could, drawing on my journalistic skills, asking my next question, striving to remain professional. It wasn't easy, but I somehow managed to hold it together.

'Okay, I think I get it, catch-22, but what *did* you do? That day Karen told you everything she did. You must have done something.'

Nicholson's expression softened. I think it was easier for him to tell this part of his story. Or, at least, that's how it seemed to me. 'I asked Karen to arrange an urgent planning meeting involving senior representatives of all the key agencies, the police, the education department, health, the council's legal department, ourselves, and any other agencies directly involved. And I asked her to do it quickly. I wanted the meeting arranged for that afternoon. And then, as soon as Karen was off the phone, I made three calls, one after another, firstly to DI Trevor Simpson, my opposite number in the police, then to Roy Evans, the director of social services, and finally to Phillip Beringer, one of my child care team managers. All the calls were important for different reasons. Some things needed to be agreed upon before the planning meeting took place.'

'Can you expand on that for me?'

Nicholson nodded.

'Okay, firstly Trevor Simpson, he was responsible for child protection for the force. He was a good man, and the children mattered to him. It wasn't just a job like it is for some people. I needed to be sure he was fully up to speed and that we were singing from the same hymn sheet. He had his doubts about Galbraith's involvement in the ring at first, purely based on reputation. But by the time we'd discussed all the available evidence, he was as convinced as I was. It was time to move things forward, time to follow the organised abuse procedures and get everything in place.

'Next came Roy Evans; I needed to be sure he was covering my back. I needed resources, and he was the man who could give them to me. By the end of our discussion, he'd agreed to me setting up a specialist team of experienced child protection social workers to investigate the ring abuse allegations and nothing else. I wanted them to concentrate on the one thing, no distractions. They'd be carefully chosen and seconded from child care teams all across the department. Appointing the right people with the right experience, temperament, and skills was crucial. And that's where Phillip Beringer fitted in. The director agreed to Phil heading up the new dedicated child protection social work team, subject to his agreement. I convinced Roy that Phil was the right man for the job. And I was to involve myself in the investigation in a supporting role, to keep a watching brief and offer advice and guidance as needed.'

I was taken aback by Nicholson's mention of Beringer. His was a name I knew well. Beringer was an old friend of my father. They were drinking buddies, long-time squash partners. I used to call him 'uncle' as a child, although we weren't related. He was friendly enough with my mother, too, in fact with the whole family. He visited our home often back then, but less so as time went on. Surely my father would have said something to him at the time of our family difficulties? Surely Beringer must have known I was due to see Galbraith? It was something else I had to explore, more questions that demanded answers.

'Did Beringer head up the team? Did that actually happen?'

'Yes, he did, I got straight on the phone to him after speaking to the director, and I wasn't at all surprised when he agreed to the role. I think, in reality, the prospect scared the life out of him. But he was never going to admit that, not to me or anyone else. That was the sort of social worker he was, determined, proudly working-class, crude at times, a bit worn around the edges. But he was sound, reliable. And that's what mattered. I was glad to have him on board.'

'And all that was agreed *before* the meeting?'

'Yes, that's right, everything had to happen quickly, and I'm talking about *very* quickly. I wanted the meeting done, everything agreed, and everything in place. There was no time for delay. There was one hell of a lot to do. We had to get on with it.'

* * *

Nicholson checked an antique brass wall clock located on the chimney breast above a glowing wood-burner. 'We can leave it there if you like, or I can tell you more. I don't mind either way. I could see you were struggling with some of the things I've told you. A lot of this stuff must come as a shock. I'll leave the decision to you.'

I didn't need to think for very long. I wanted the whole picture. My following query provided Nicholson with his answer.

'What happened at the meeting?'

'Fancy another coffee before we continue?'

I took my chance, grabbing at the opportunity for a drink. 'Have you got a beer?'

Nicholson stood, smiled thinly and nodded. 'Lager or bitter?'

My relief was so intense as to seem almost tangible. That's not an easy thing to admit, but it's true. I'd never wanted anything more. 'Lager, please, chilled if you've got it, don't bother with a glass.'

Nicholson left the room, but was back in under a minute. He handed me a cold can, opening a second himself.

'Are you ready?'

I took a second generous slurp, swilling the amber liquid around my mouth before swallowing with a satisfied sigh. I placed the can to one side, careful not to spill a single drop, and then poised my pen above my notepad. Nicholson patiently waited until I was ready.

'How much detail do you want, Tony? Give me an idea.'

'Everything you can tell me.'

'Okay, as long as I know. The meeting went ahead at three o'clock sharp. Everybody who needed to be there was there, and we agreed on how to take things forward, with the police and social services taking the lead as investigative agencies. Phillip Beringer would head up the social work team with day-to-day management responsibility for the case. Trevor Simpson would lead a similarly dedicated police team, liaising with Phil to agree on joint action as necessary. Phil would also liaise with the council solicitors and two consultant paediatricians with experience in cases of sexual abuse. Trevor Simpson would do the same with the Crown Prosecution Service, and I'd act as a consultant, a sounding board and source of advice to everyone involved, if and when they needed it. I appreciate that all sounds simple enough, but it took some agreement.'

I took a third generous swig of lager, emptying the can in one greedy swallow. 'Why was that?'

'Some of the attendees reacted much as you did.'

'I'm not with you.'

'The idea of allowing Galbraith to continue working as a child psychiatrist for as long as was necessary was hard for some to accept. They wanted the health authority formally notified that day and Galbraith suspended immediately. I completely get that.

Of course I do. It would have been wonderful had that been possible. But that one simple act would have completely wrecked the investigation. Trevor Simpson wasn't having any of it. He made it crystal clear that he didn't want Galbraith or anyone else warned because premature action would seriously jeopardise a complex criminal investigation. And he stressed the word *criminal*. He didn't want anyone left in any doubt. If the authorities acted too quickly or confidential information was leaked, many more children would suffer. And offenders, predatory criminals guilty of heinous offences, would escape justice.'

I placed my empty can to one side, nodding as Nicholson continued.

'I'd never seen or heard anything like it. Trevor was on his feet, pointing at people, jabbing a finger, demanding their attention. He even went as far as to meet the eyes of each potential dissenter in turn and tell them in no uncertain terms that if *anyone* broke confidence, if anyone said a single word that potentially compromised the investigation, he'd arrest them for attempting to pervert the course of justice. I've got to be honest; I was shocked. And everyone else was too. I could see it on their faces. But it was *exactly* what the case needed. It wouldn't have worked otherwise. I shook Trevor's hand and thanked him after the meeting. I think he saved the day. There was only one way we were ever going to succeed. We had to interview all the children already in care, gather what evidence we could, including medical examinations when appropriate, and then progress from there.'

I nodded again for him to continue.

'The police would then make coordinated arrests as soon as the CPS decided there was sufficient evidence to make the charges stick. And any children in the care of the identified offenders would be interviewed and medically examined immediately following the arrests. It couldn't come quickly enough. But we couldn't put a timescale on it. We had to get on with it, do everything by the book, and hope for the best.

'There were ten police officers involved initially and a similar number of social workers, with others joining the teams as and when necessary. We knew we couldn't save all the children involved, however much we wanted to. I do realise that sounds awful, but we didn't even know who some of them were. We'd try to gather more information at every opportunity, but it was never going to be perfect. And it was the same for the offenders. We knew the identity of some but not others. We knew it was virtually impossible to get all of them. But we were going to do our very best to try. Nailing any of them was going to be a challenge. We knew that from the start.'

I made my final notes before packing my briefcase, preparing to leave. I could see Nicholson had said enough. And I'd heard enough, too, more than enough for one day.

'How the hell did you cope?'

'I wonder that myself sometimes. But I didn't have a choice. It wasn't easy for any of us. I saw investigative staff in tears, police officers as well as social workers. And others did much more than me. I want to stress that. Please include that in your book. I did my bit, but it was the frontline workers who did the hard graft. They talked to the kids, they obtained the evidence, they made the arrests, not the senior managers. It's with them that the credit lies.'

I rose to my feet, shaking Nicholson's hand with what I hoped was warmth and affection. I felt genuine respect for the man. While I couldn't bring myself to agree with everything he'd done back then, I did at least understand the rationale. He'd explained himself well.

'Can I contact you again, at a later date, if I need to know more? I'd really appreciate it if I could.'

He took a deep breath on opening the front door, exhaling slowly. It wasn't the first time, and I'm sure it won't be the last. It's a coping mechanism I use myself. 'Give me a ring, and we'll sort something out.'

My head was aching, and I needed another drink. I pictured a whisky in my hand. It called out to me. I could almost taste it. I thanked Nicholson profusely and headed to my car.

13

The unexpected revelation regarding Phillip Beringer's involvement in the investigation of the organised abuse ring, with Galbraith at its centre, was at the forefront of my mind as I drove away from Nicholson's comfortable home. The idea that a man who knew my family and me so well, a man my parents considered a close friend, might have chosen not to act to protect me from the foul attentions of the predatory doctor left me both angry and confused. There was always the possibility that Beringer might have been unaware that I was one of Galbraith's patients or that a further appointment was pending, but that seemed unlikely. He and my father were close, and they spent a lot of time together. If my father had discussed our family problems with anyone, it would have been Beringer. I pondered events as I drove in the direction of home, eventually deciding to talk to my father first rather than go direct to Beringer.

It had been a long time since I'd seen Beringer, years in fact. I didn't have his contact details, so I couldn't text or ring him. And I couldn't find any sign of him on social media. Turning up on his doorstep unannounced, demanding explanations about events now long gone, was unlikely to go well. I would interview Beringer; I was determined about that, I wanted answers. But I planned to ask my father to facilitate the meeting, maybe even be there himself, if that was Beringer's preferred option. That wouldn't be my first choice, but I was willing to compromise to make the interview happen.

* * *

I met my father in a quiet corner of a local rugby club, popular with locals, at a little after seven on the evening of that same day. We were both familiar with the club, and it was somewhere we were comfortable. I'd trained there as a child, played for the youth team. People knew me, and I knew them.

My father was sitting alone at a small table behind the worn-out pool table when I entered the bar, nestling a half-empty pint of brown ale in both hands as if he was wary of someone snatching it from him at any moment. There were two empty smoky bacon crisp packets and a sodden beermat on the table in front of him. The entire scene looked almost as timeworn as he did. He looked up with tired eyes, nodding as I walked towards him, but he didn't say anything in greeting. My father isn't a man of many words when sober. Why say hello when a nod would suffice? I knew that our conversation wouldn't be easy for him. Talking of anything other than the mundane banalities of life would be something of a challenge he'd no doubt prefer to avoid. Maybe another drink or two would help. It usually did.

I stood immediately in front of him, my black leather briefcase held loosely in one hand by the handle. 'Another pint, Dad?'

He tilted his head back, sank his beer in two seconds flat, and then handed me the empty glass without a single word. I could see that his hand was trembling ever so slightly as he reached out.

And he avoided my eyes, which surprised me. His usual assured confidence appeared to have slipped away. It seemed the stress was getting to him, as it was to me. Maybe I hadn't fully considered the impact of my writing on others, particularly those close to me. I made a mental commitment to be more sensitive to the feelings of my family. They lived many of the events of my past too. I placed my briefcase under the table next to one of two empty chairs before heading to the bar.

Even the attractive brown-haired barmaid's low-cut top and ample cleavage weren't sufficient to raise my flagging spirits as I ordered two pints, another brown ale for my father and a strong German lager for me. I thanked her, paid in cash, and joined my father at the table. An old Rolling Stones hit from the sixties was playing on the wall-mounted jukebox. We sat opposite each other, both downing close to half our pints in one generous swallow before my father was the first to speak.

'What's this about, son? I know you're doing this book thing. But you've talked to your mother. Talk to her again if you need to. I don't know anything that she doesn't. She's better at this stuff than me. You know how it is.'

I emptied my glass down my throat. He was nothing if not predictable. 'Phillip Beringer!'

My father jerked his head back. 'Phil, what about him?'

'I want to interview him.'

He took another slurp of beer, wiped his mouth with his hand. A dribble ran down his chin. 'Good luck with that; he's visiting his sister in New Zealand, won't be back for another two weeks.'

I picked up both empty glasses, returned to the bar, and then to our table, where I handed him his next drink, which he accepted gratefully. He's never one to turn down a pint. Something it seems we have in common.

'Okay, so he's away, that's not a problem. I want you to arrange for me to talk to Phil as soon as he's back, but for now, you're going to have to do. There are questions I need answering. Things that can't wait.'

My father's displeasure couldn't have been more obvious. It was painted all over his face. 'Oh, come off it, Tony. I know your generation is into this touchy-feely, heart on your sleeve, sharing your feelings crap. But wouldn't you be better off leaving this shit in the past? You've got to look to the future, move on with your life. The past is gone. Forget it, that's always been my philosophy. Live in the now.'

If only it were that simple! I opened my briefcase, taking out my notepad and pen. I'd never felt more determined. He wasn't wheedling his way out of this one. He had a story to tell, and I was going to hear it.

'I'm going to ask the questions, and you're going to answer them. You owe me that much. If you hadn't walked out on us all those years ago, I'd never even have met Galbraith. Answering a few questions is the least you can do.'

The look on my father's face told me I'd said too much; thinned lips, flared nostrils and a chin that pushed up and out. His angry exasperation couldn't have been clearer. 'I know I fucked up. I'm fully aware of that. I'm not a complete idiot, and I don't need reminding. But your mother and me got back together. She forgave me. And it was thirty fucking years ago! Let it go, Tony! Give me a break, for fuck's sake; enough's enough.'

I wasn't used to him swearing, or at least, not as much as that. It wasn't the first time, but it was unusual. Both his use of language and the intensity of his statement shook me. I hadn't expected such a strong emotional reaction. I chose my following words with care. 'Look, I know you couldn't *possibly* have known what it would lead to when you left Mum for Tina. I don't blame you for my encountering Galbraith. But it happened. I need to understand the events of that time. We're different that way. I can't just pretend none of it happened. That's what this is all about. My research has left me with unanswered questions about Phil's involvement. I'm hoping you can help me fill in the gaps.'

He looked away momentarily before returning his attention to me. 'Okay, let's get this over with. What do you want to know?'

'Did you tell Phil about the clinic? Did he know I was referred to Galbraith by the GP?'

My father took another slurp of beer, but he didn't wipe his mouth this time. 'Yeah, I told him, one night in the pub after a few drinks. I told him I regretted moving in with Tina. And I mentioned the clinic. I wasn't too enthusiastic about you continuing the treatment. I knew Phil worked with kids and all that, so I asked him what he thought. I didn't think it would do you any good, and Phil said he thought the same way. I knew nothing about the ring at that point or Phil's involvement. I didn't have a clue Galbraith was being investigated, not then. Phil kept all that to himself.'

'You said *continuing my treatment*, not starting, *continuing*; when did you first tell Phil about the clinic? I want you to think carefully, the *when* matters.'

My father stood stiffly, headed to the bar, laughed along with the barmaid in response to some joke or other, and then returned to our table carrying our drinks and two more packets of crisps.

'What were you asking?'

I tried to be patient, repeating myself. 'When, Dad, *when* did you tell him?'

'It was just a couple of days before the second appointment, the one I didn't go to. It was just you and your mother.'

I now knew that Beringer was fully aware of the dangers I faced when my father talked to him in the pub that night. There was no room for ambiguity, no room for doubt. I took another drink, savouring the golden liquid before swallowing. I thought of it as medicine, taking the edge off, helping me cope. I don't think I've ever felt so let down. I wanted to talk to Beringer face-to-face, to challenge him up close and personal. But for now, my father would have to do. 'How did Phil react when you told him? Did he say anything?'

'Yeah, he went white, he said he didn't think the clinic was a good idea, that he'd have a word with Mum to try to talk her out of it. It seemed like an overreaction. I hadn't seen him like that before. Of course, once I knew the full facts, it all made sense. But it didn't at the time. He was in a right state. I appealed to him as a friend. I asked him if there was anything he wasn't telling me, but he denied it. And then he said he was feeling ill. I followed him as far as the door. He puked up in the car park before driving off.'

I wasn't ready to let it go. 'But did he say *why* he didn't think the clinic was a good idea? Did he say anything about the dangers posed by Galbraith? Anything at all?'

'No, of course he didn't, fuck all! If he had, I'd have done something about it. Do you *really* think I'd have let you go to that second appointment if he had? I knew nothing about Galbraith's crimes. I only found out the cunt was a nonce when I saw it on the news weeks later. Phil's involvement in Galbraith's investigation came as a complete shock to me, too. I couldn't believe he hadn't told me or your mother. I thought we were better friends than that. We were both gobsmacked when we found out the reality.'

My father was red in the face, sweating. I made some written notes, buying time to think, considering my next question, allowing him to catch his breath. He was panting slightly. I could see the pressure was getting to him. But I wasn't sure I believed him, not entirely, not all of it.

'Okay, I hear what you're saying, but I've got to be sure. Did you know that Phil was involved in the organised abuse investigation before my second appointment? He was managing the investigative team. It had all just happened. It must have been a big deal for him. Is that something he talked to you about?'

My father's dark expression said a thousand words. '*No*, Tony, *no*! I've already told you, Phil told me fuck all! If he had, I might have put two and two together. Your behaviour had improved after the first appointment. Phil said that was nothing to do with Galbraith, that you just needed time. He rang your mum at home and said the same thing to her. But she wouldn't listen. She thought I'd put Phil up to it to get my way. And I was the last person she'd listen to back then. If anything, she seemed even more determined to go after Phil's call. Neither me nor your mum knew anything significant at that time, fuck all, that *all* came later. Phil kept his secrets to himself.'

'Did you ever ask Beringer why he didn't spell it out for you in time to stop the second appointment going ahead? You know, a quiet word in your ear, make certain Tony doesn't see Galbraith under any circumstances, he's under investigation, that kind of thing.'

'Ask him? Of course, I fucking well asked him! I stormed around his place as soon as I found out he must have known. It was all over the media by then, the TV, the newspapers. I punched him in the face hard, broke his nose.'

I laughed despite myself. I hadn't thought my father was capable of such things. But a part of me was glad he was. His actions told me the events of that time mattered to him, too, that he'd cared.

'How did Phil react? Did he give you any explanations?'

'He was sitting on the floor holding his face and choking on his blood at the time. He just kept saying he was sorry in between swallowing. I didn't hang about to listen to any more of his shit. Nothing he could have said was going to make me feel any better. If I'd stayed there, I'd have hit him again. It was weeks until we spoke after that and months before I considered him a friend. But I was missing him, that's the truth of it. When he rang me asking if I wanted a game of squash followed by a few pints, I said yes. We never spoke of Galbraith again.'

'What, never?'

'No, as I say, I moved on.'

'Until now!'

He downed his beer and grinned. 'Yeah, thanks for that. Do you still want to talk to Phil, or are you done?'

'I want to talk to him, now more than ever.'

'I'll sort it out as soon as he's back in town.'

'Another pint?'

He seemed to relax for the first time that evening. 'I thought you'd never ask. I'll have another brown ale and a whisky chaser, make it a double. I can leave the car in the car park and get a taxi home. Your mother won't be expecting me until late.'

I decided to do likewise, sobriety could wait for another day.

14

I talked to Detective Sergeant Pam Forsyth while sitting next to her on a wooden bench close to a Victorian bandstand in the local park. She turned up to meet me wearing a bright red track-suit trimmed with white, her slightly greying mousey hair pulled back in a tight ponytail secured with a matching red ribbon that caught the winter sun. She was cheery, approachable and friendly, but there was a discernible air of sadness about her, too. A feeling of sorrow that I suspect stemmed from her anticipation of what we were about to discuss. She told me that she'd been running, an antidote to stress she'd adopted at the time of the organised abuse investigation. A habit she continued to this day. She looked fit and younger than her years. The exercise was clearly doing her some good. Maybe I should take it up myself I thought.

After a couple of minutes of general chit-chat, the detective sergeant moved on to tell me of an interview she and senior social work practitioner – Alan Garret, conducted with a young primary school girl, who I'll call Susan for the sake of the story. By a strange coincidence, the interview took place on the exact same date as my second appointment at the child guidance clinic. The criminal intelligence related to Galbraith was building. The police were getting closer, but sadly, still not quickly enough for me.

Susan's evidence provided corroboration rather than revelation, in terms of both the genuinely shocking size of the organised abuse ring and the heinous nature of the numerous offences committed against far too many child victims. Like other children before her, Susan talked of being taken to a barn-like farm building where multiple men assaulted her sexually. She'd experienced too much and seen too much in her short life of unutterable trauma. She'd suffered herself and seen many other children, some younger than herself, subjected to unspeakable horrors at the hands of their various abusers. She described those many offences in the detail required for evidence, assaults of all kinds, including rape. Susan also mentioned Galbraith by name, ever so quietly, ever so reticently, as if fearing he might overhear her. She described him as the boss, and the criminal group as Pet Club, as Gary Davies had during my visit to Swansea Prison.

The sergeant's upset was written all over her face as she told me the detail of the young girl's allegations. Every such offence the officer dealt with, both then and since, had left her horrified as to the sexual harm offenders like those described by Susan chose to inflict on their victims. She asked me why men would commit such horrors, saying they were worse than animals. She asked me the same question again when I didn't reply. I didn't have an answer.

* * *

My research has taught me some perpetrators were abused as children, but the vast majority were not. And to say it's all about power seems an inadequate cliché. Power may well be a factor, but it's not the whole picture. There *has to* be more to it than that. I'm glad I don't understand. I thank God that I don't understand. I can't think of anything worse than having any commonality with them.

DS Forsyth told me she had nothing but respect and admiration for Susan and other children like her. Susan had been so keen to put her allegations on the record, so determined to tell her story, both in the interests of justice and that of her siblings. She was prepared to go on record and give evidence in court, however arduous the questioning by her abusers' legal counsel. And she was ready to do all that at such a young age. I find that as incredible now as the officer did then.

I asked the detective sergeant how she coped with such work, the responsibility, the emotional and psychological distress. She looked me in the eye and simply replied that she didn't. She told me of an incident where she'd vomited after one particularly harrowing interview related to the ring. Running became a lifeline, a means of survival. DS Forsyth left the police child protection unit when it reached a point where she could no longer function in her professional and private life. She was allocated alternative duties after an extended period of sick leave and never returned to child protection. She's now part of the force training department and happy with that.

I asked her if she'd like to read the book if and when it's published. She told me that she wouldn't, that the memories it engendered would be too vivid, too raw, even after so long. But she did ask one favour of me before we separated that day. She wanted me to dedicate the book to survivors everywhere. A small but important gesture I'm happy to fulfil. And I'll raise a glass to them, too, when I next get the opportunity. I wish them nothing but the best, every one. They deserve no less.

15

The interview with Phillip Beringer was scheduled for sooner than I'd anticipated. My father bumped into him in town and let me know. I don't know if he was back in Wales due to an earlier than planned return from his travels or if my father simply got the dates wrong. And to be honest, I don't care. I didn't ask Beringer his reasons, and I don't plan to. I entered his ground-floor flat with my briefcase in hand, glad to escape the winter chill. There were important things to discuss. I needed answers. I was determined he'd provide them.

I hadn't seen Beringer for quite some time before that day. He was looking older than I remembered him as a child, greyer, heavier, with a beer gut hanging over the waistband of his over-tight trousers. He was unshaven, unkempt, with dark skin around both eyes. I almost felt sorry for him, this shadow of the man I'd known, but only almost. There was far too much historical baggage for sympathy. He allowed the doorframe to support his weight for a few seconds before finally inviting me in.

'What can I do for you, Tony? Long time, no see.'

I followed him into a sparsely furnished lounge that looked long past its best, not unlike him. 'Didn't my father tell you?'

He flopped into a purple armchair with his bare feet resting on a teak coffee table fashionable in the 1970s.

'Well, he mumbled something about you writing a book. But I only heard half of it. The old ears aren't what they were these days. Not much of me is.'

Beringer lowered his feet to the floor, sitting upright, staring at me when I explained the reasons for the book, my reasons for the visit. It was as if he was trying to read my thoughts, fearing the worst. There was a conciliatory tone to his voice when he finally spoke. 'I've been dreading this for thirty long years. I knew one day you'd come knocking on my door. I guess that day's finally come. Best get it over with, don't you think? Say what you've got to say and go.'

I held my hands out wide, palms forward, fingers spread. 'Why, Phil? You knew the danger I was in; Galbraith was an animal. You could have helped me. You spoke to Mum and Dad. You could have told them how dangerous Galbraith was, the three of you were friends. You could have protected me, but you didn't. Why didn't you do more?'

Beringer dropped his chin to his chest. 'Do you think I didn't want to? I was caught in a shit storm. You've got no idea of the pressure I was under; you've never done the sort of work I did. You couldn't hope to understand.'

'Try me, Phil. I'm here, and I'm ready to listen. Tell me what happened, explain yourself.'

He was silent for a second or two, seemingly pondering his response. 'If I do this, that's it, yeah? I need to know you're not going to come back. I want this done and dusted. This one visit, one interview, and that's it, no more knocking on my door. Take it or leave it. That's the only deal I'm offering.'

I reluctantly agreed to his terms. I don't think he'd have talked if I hadn't. I switched on the recorder, waiting for him to start.

'I'd just been asked to head up a social work team to investigate the organised abuse ring. It was big, a major case with multiple offenders and even more victims. It wasn't like anything I'd dealt with before. Failure was unthinkable; I was crapping myself, the pressure was horrendous. And then, if that wasn't bad enough, your father told me you were seeing Galbraith at the clinic. You'd been once and were about to go again. I wanted to tell your father what kind of man Galbraith was, of the danger you were in, but you know what your father was like, he had a big mouth, particularly after a drink. If I'd told him, the whole world would have known about it. He wouldn't have kept his mouth shut. The entire investigation would have been compromised before I'd even started. I couldn't risk that. There was too much at stake. My career was on the line. And if those abusing bastards had been pre-warned something was up, they could have got away with it. The ring might have continued for years. Hundreds more kids could have suffered if I hadn't kept my mouth shut.'

I'd expected something along the lines of what he'd said. I knew he'd try to justify his inaction. But it wasn't nearly good enough, not for me. 'So, I was collateral damage. Is that what you're saying? Your job was more important than I was. You did nothing to help me.'

'I didn't do *nothing*, Tony. I lost sleep. I did what I could. Your dad wasn't too keen on you going to the clinic, so I told him he was right, that you didn't need that sort of intervention, that he should dump that new girl in his life and get back with your mum. And I tried to influence your mother too. I did my very best to convince her that the clinic wasn't a good idea without actually telling her the truth of why. I told her I had a lot of experience dealing with the kind of issues she was experiencing and that things would get better given time. But she didn't want to hear it. The more I said, the more irritated she became. She thought your father had put me up to it. I knew it was a lost cause by the end.'

'And then you just let me fall into Galbraith's clutches as if I was worthless.'

'No, Tony, that is *not* what happened, not even close. I talked it through with a mate of mine, a bloke I trained with, a child protection manager who worked in a different part of the country. And we came up with a plan. Your father was due to run you and your mother to the clinic first thing on the morning of the second appointment. I knew the date, and I knew the time. So, in the early hours, I punctured all four of your father's car tyres. I know that sounds insane, it does to me even now, but I didn't know what the hell else I could do. I was just buying some time. I thought your appointment would be cancelled and rearranged, and maybe, just maybe, Galbraith would be arrested by the time you were due to see him again.'

'But it didn't work out that way.'

'No, it didn't, and I'm sorry about that, but I did my best. I couldn't have done more, not in the exceptional circumstances. What I did was the wrong choice for you but not for others. And there were a lot of them, a great many kids in need of protection. They were in danger too. I couldn't risk fucking all that up for your sake, however much I wanted to. I had no choice but to look at the bigger picture. And that wasn't easy to do. It made me feel like shit. I ended up on antidepressants. Things aren't always black and white. I was dealing with shades of grey. It still affects me to this day.'

I closed my notepad, returning it to my briefcase. 'Are you sure you did your best, really, even now when you look back on it with me sitting here? You don't sound too convinced to me.'

He struggled to his feet, supporting his bulk with the arm of his chair. 'It's time to go, Tony. We're finished here. I've said all I'm going to say.'

I could see the anguish on Beringer's face, the depth with which he regretted the events that shaped, not only my life, but his. And so, I shook his hand before leaving. He's not a bad man. He was misguided rather than evil. And grudges serve no purpose. They eat away at you. It was time to let it go.

16

As I sat at my desk this afternoon, my laptop at the ready, I realised I've been doing anything and everything to avoid writing this part of my story. My second appointment at the child guidance clinic was somewhat traumatic, and that's putting it mildly. It isn't easy to revisit that caustic period of my life. But I have to face it. I have to look the devil in the eye. It's time to get this done. What's the point of the book otherwise?

This chapter is heavily based on another interview with my mother, although my childhood memories also inform the narrative. Our conversation again took place at the family cottage. It was a cold winter day, the kitchen chilly even with the central heating on. My mother, wrapped in a thick red wool shawl, made us both hot, sweet peppermint tea before we began. She handed me my cup filled to the brim, sat herself down with a slight groan, and started talking.

'I'm not looking forward to this.'

'I'm grateful to you for doing it.'

'I've been giving a lot of thought to the time between the first and second appointments at the clinic.'

I blew on my tea, cooling it before sipping. 'I was hoping you had. I've been doing the same myself.'

'It was an extremely difficult and emotional time. I need you to understand that. Your father had started telling me how much he regretted the affair, that he wanted us to get back together, and that he'd only moved in with Tina because I'd kicked him out. He kept saying you'd be fine if we resolved our differences, that the last thing you needed was a head doctor. But he was still living with the tart. He always had a way of oversimplifying things that wasn't helpful.'

'Is that why you went ahead with the second appointment?'

She emitted a long, deep, audible breath. 'I knew there was some truth in what your father was saying. But I was confused, conflicted. It was all very well for Dad to say you'd be fine if we kissed and made up. But we hadn't; we were so very far from that. He was still living with the girl he'd left me for. She was so much younger than me, all make-up, long legs, high heels, and very short skirts. My self-confidence was shattered. I needed action, not words. And you seemed so much better after that first appointment. There'd been a definite improvement in your behaviour; you were still wetting the bed from time to time, but it wasn't every night as it had been. And you'd started retaking an interest in sports. That was a huge relief, and I thought things were looking up.'

I tilted my head at a slight angle. 'Why do you think things had been so much better?'

'Looking back, I think all that was very likely down to your father spending more time with you. He was giving you more attention, showing more interest. And your father and I were talking again. It wasn't all heated arguments. That gave you hope. All that's clear to me now. It seems obvious. But at the time, I put the positive changes in your mood and behaviour down to the doctor. I didn't know what Galbraith had done to help so very much, but I thought that he had. I wasn't sure what to do for the best.'

She clasped her tea in her hands and continued. 'I even had Phillip Beringer on the phone, telling me the appointment wasn't a good idea. He kept repeating himself, but he didn't seem to be able to tell me why he thought I should cancel. It annoyed the hell out of me. In the end, I just thought your father had put him up to it. They did a lot of drinking together. I think Phil was drunk when he rang.

'If anything, his call made me more determined to keep the second appointment. I eventually decided it was the right thing for you, and if I'm honest, I didn't want your father to get his way; there'd been more than enough of that already. Of course, later on, when I found out the real reason for Phil's call, how much he knew, how much he kept from me, I was completely furious. All he had to do was be honest, but, no, he couldn't do it. We were supposed to be friends. I expected better. Had I known the full facts, that second appointment would never have happened. Who knows? Maybe then we wouldn't be sitting here now.'

I could see the strained emotion in my mother's eyes as she brushed non-existent fluff from a sleeve, waiting for my response.

'I spoke to Phil yesterday, as it happens.'

'Really?'

'He knows he let us all down. He knows he should have said more. But he still tried to justify himself. He tried to explain away his inaction as if anything he said could make it better.'

'He's not someone I could ever forgive.'

'I don't think he's ever forgiven himself.'

She rose stiffly to her feet. 'I need a break, Tony. I could do with an aspirin. Can you give me five minutes?'

'Take as long as you need.'

* * *

I could see that she'd been crying again when she returned to her seat. She's been doing a lot of that lately, which I do appreciate is largely down to me. 'Are you okay to go on, Mum?'

She nodded once. 'We've got this far. Let's get it over with.'

'What happened that morning – the morning of the appointment?'

'It was a cold morning, even colder than today. I'd struggled to sleep. I got up early, pulled on one of your father's old red rugby shirts, and headed downstairs, making sure not to wake you and Siân. I needed a bit of me-time before facing what I knew was going to be a stressful day. As it turned out, it was infinitely worse than I ever imagined. It would have been better if I hadn't got up at all.'

I'd found Beringer's claims about damaging my father's car less than convincing. It's not how I recalled events. I was keen to check the facts. 'Am I right in thinking Dad picked us up in the convertible?'

She let out an indignant snort. 'He was supposed to. But he wasn't the most reliable man in the world. I rang him early that morning to make sure he was up, and then got you two out of bed to get dressed and have breakfast before he arrived. The agreed plan was he'd pick us up with enough time to drop Siân off at school on the way to the clinic. And then, when I could see things were running late, he rang *claiming* someone had vandalised his car. He said he'd only found out five minutes before.'

So Beringer had told me the truth. At least now I knew. 'They had – it was Phil. All four tyres were slashed.'

Her mouth fell open. 'Really?'

'Yes, really, Phil told me that himself. It was his cack-handed way of trying to stop the appointment going ahead.'

'My God, I didn't know that until now. I thought it was your father trying to get out of taking us. It was the sort of thing he'd do. I didn't believe half the things he said in those days.'

I realised my recollections of that morning weren't as complete as I'd thought. Memories don't come in straight lines. To some extent, we rewrite our past, and not always for the better.

'So, how *did* we get to the clinic?'

'I told your father to order a taxi and to meet us here as fast as he possibly could. I had about fifty pence in my purse. My calling one wasn't an option. And you couldn't pay by card back then. I could see there was no way to get to the appointment on time, so I rang the clinic. That Sharon you interviewed answered the phone. I told her what was happening and that we'd get there as soon as we could. But she said we'd have to make an alternative appointment, cancel the one we had and rearrange.'

'I thought we went that day.'

My mother nodded twice, brushing a strand of hair away from her eyes, blinking it away. 'Oh, we did, more's the pity. I persuaded her to speak to the doctor on our behalf, apologise, and ask him if he'd still see us. I didn't beg for her help, but it was pretty damned close. I was pleased when she finally agreed to try. How wrong can a mother be?'

'And, of course, Galbraith was only too willing to see us. I bet he was champing at the bit.'

'Yes, the phone went quiet for a short time, and then I heard Sharon's voice again, saying to bring you in. I thanked her. I actually thanked her. I was so grateful at the time, more fool me.'

'You couldn't have known.' How many times did I have to say it? Who's making *me* feel better? It seems I've got to do that for myself.

'The taxi arrived about ten minutes later, with your father sitting in the front passenger seat next to the driver. Siân had caught a bus for school by that time, so it was just you and me sitting in the back.'

The more she said, the more I remembered. 'Was the taxi bright red?'

'Yes, I think it was. One of those French cars, a Citroen or a Peugeot, I can't remember which.'

Ah, so I did remember after all. It was all flooding back. 'What happened when we got to the clinic?'

'Your father stayed in the car when we got out. And then he wound the window down to ask me if I wanted him to go in with us. I could tell how relieved he was when I said no. Your father is nothing if not predictable. I told him I wanted him back there with a taxi in an hour to pick us up. He couldn't get away quickly enough.'

'What happened when we first went into the clinic? I've got my own recollections, but I want to hear it from you.'

'I could see Galbraith for a brief moment looking at us through the blinds in his office as we walked towards the entrance.'

'I bet he was!'

My mother shrugged, raising and lowering her shoulders. 'Well, obviously, it's chilling now when we know the facts. But I found it strangely reassuring at the time. I thought he was keen to help us. That he was interested in your wellbeing, and then he came rushing out into the car park as we were approaching the door. He stopped dead, watching the taxi drive away, and then said he'd wanted a word with your father before he left. Galbraith seemed less composed than I'd seen him before, flustered even. But I didn't read anything into it. I certainly didn't have any suspicions. The thought that he might be a sex offender never crossed my mind. That sort of thing wasn't even on my radar in those days. It was a more trusting time. I told him your dad would be back in an hour. He seemed satisfied with that and then turned his attention to you.'

'To me, how?'

'It's strange how some pictures stick in your mind. I can still see it as if I was there only this morning. Galbraith patted you on the back with the palm of his right hand. And then he became his usual exuberant, charming self, creating a character, playing to the gallery, drawing us in. Give me a second; I want to get the words right. What was it he said? Yes, that was it. He focused on you first and then on me. He asked how you were, said he'd been waiting for your arrival.'

'Oh, he'd been waiting, all right! Waiting with his mouth watering.'

'And then he said he had a nice box of chocolates in his desk drawer with your name on it. He asked me what I thought, whether you could have some treats. He called them treats, not sweets or chocolates, treats.'

'First the sherbet lemons and then the chocolates. It was obviously a tactic he used, one of many. Whatever worked best in the circumstances.'

My mother began slowly drumming the tabletop with the fingers of her right hand as the memories stung and festered. 'I remember taking your hand as Galbraith led us into reception. He was directing the orchestra, and I can see that now. He told us to wait in his office while he had a word with his secretary. I could overhear the conversation. He asked her to deliver a report by hand to somewhere or other, said it was urgent.'

I swallowed hard, then let out a breath. The memories were flooding back as clear as day. 'It was the scheming bastard's way of getting her out of the building. He wanted her gone, you gone, and me on my own.'

My mother nodded. 'He told her not to rush back, to ensure

she enjoyed a lovely lunch before returning. I remember thinking what a nice boss he was. How lucky she was to be working with such a thoughtful man.' Mother shook her head slowly, first one way, then the other. 'That makes me feel utterly ridiculous now. How could I misread the situation so very badly? I thought he was one of the nicest men I'd ever met. My God! It couldn't have been further from the truth.'

'He was good at what he did, Mum. We saw what he wanted us to see. He created a character, props and all.'

'And then he joined us in his office, all smiles, all nice reassuring words. He told me how wonderful it was to see me, and he thanked me for coming, but then he said there was no reason for me to stay, as if it was the most obvious thing in the world. He kept calling me his dear girl and saying that you'd be *fine* in his care. He repeated that at least twice more as if trying to convince me. As if he knew the thought of leaving you wasn't sitting comfortably.'

'What happened next?'

'I can remember standing there, not quite sure what to do even after everything he'd said, but then he told me I could collect you in an hour. He took the box of chocolates he'd mentioned from a drawer, allowed you to take one, and then insisted I take some before leaving. "Take a handful before you go, my dear girl. Go on, take some. Why not spoil yourself? What do you say, Anthony? Should Mum take some treats before she leaves us together?"'

I remembered those poisonous words almost as well as my mother did. I could hear Galbraith saying them as my mother spoke. His voice, not hers, rang in my ears. I could see his face. Then, all of a sudden, he was gone again. I was back in the room. 'He'd got rid of Sharon, and now he was getting rid of you, too,' I said.

'You took another chocolate, popped it in your mouth and started chewing. You seemed surprisingly relaxed, happy in his company. And I walked away, I left you there, with *that man*. I'm so very sorry for that. It's my life's biggest regret.'

There she was again with the regrets, so full of apologies. It was almost exhausting, but I knew where it came from, how the guilt tortured her. 'I know you're sorry, Mum, you don't need to keep saying it. I thought if I talked to Galbraith, you and Dad might get back together. You said the doctor was going to have a nice chat with me and that you'd be back before I knew it. It didn't seem so bad. And then you said Dad might take us both for a burger once the appointment was over. I was happy to cooperate. That sealed the deal.'

She cradled her cup in front of her with both hands, her fingers linked, I suspect appreciating the residual warmth. 'I gave you a nervous smile, then hurried from the clinic. Even then, there was something that made me anxious about leaving you. Galbraith followed me as far as the exit, watching as I crossed the car park. He waved when I glanced back.'

'And then he locked the door.'

'Yes, yes, he did, although I didn't know that at the time.'

'Of course not. How could you?'

* * *

'It was a nice sunny day, unusually pleasant for the time of year. So, I decided to walk as far as the park. Your father and I used to go there when we were courting years before. There were winter plants and a duck pond. I thought it would help the time pass more quickly. And I thought you were going to be okay. That's what I told myself. Galbraith had said as much so many times. *He'll be fine. He'll be fine.* I wanted to believe him. He almost had me convinced.'

'The bastard was still charm itself when you first left,' I told her. 'He said he had things to do before we talked. I was well pleased when he told me to go into the therapy room to choose a video to watch. He wanted me to choose the film and put the TV and video player on myself. That was all part of it. I had to have done everything, not him, me.'

Mother's brow furrowed. 'Galbraith was a monster. I'd like to have torn him limb from limb.'

'He handed me the box of chocolates before guiding me towards the therapy room, an arm around my shoulder. And then he patted my head before leaving me there, saying I should choose a film we could watch together when he returned a minute or two later.'

'Why haven't you ever said anything about this before?'

'The time never seemed right.'

'I'm glad you're telling me now. I can share the burden. We can go forward together.'

'I stuffed a couple of chocolates in my mouth and started sorting through the videos. There was nothing I'd want to watch except one, a best goals compilation. He knew that. It was planned. The bastard knew exactly which one I'd choose. I switched the TV on, took the video from its box, placed it in the VCR and pressed the play button. And then, oh my God, what a shock! When the film eventually came onto the screen, I couldn't believe what I was seeing. I was seven, for goodness' sake! It wasn't football. I stared at the screen, horrified but unable to look away as images of hard-core, violent pornography played in front of me. In the film, there was a boy, men in masks, men doing vile, terrible, horrible things. I can remember weeping, bursting into floods of tears, repeatedly calling for you. And then, just when I was as my lowest, Galbraith threw the door open, bursting into the room, twitching, sweating, red in the face, all feigned righteous indignation. I kept calling for you, asking where you were, but he was only ever going to talk about that film. The *bastard*! The vile predatory *bastard*!'

My mother reached out to comfort me. I could see her shaking, not just her hand, her entire body. I can only begin to imagine how I'd feel if Olivia experienced such horrors. Mother's focus bounced from one part of the room to another, unable to settle.

'Do you need to take a break, Tony? Maybe that's enough for one day?'

I ignored her and continued. 'The bastard stood in front of the television, looking at the screen as the two hooded men continued beating the boy, blood everywhere. I was so very relieved when he finally switched it off. But then things took an even darker turn. He told me I shouldn't have watched the film, that it wasn't good, that it wasn't good at all.

'I called out for you again, crouching on the floor, hugging my knees to my chest as he stood over me. And then he said he'd thought of something terrible, something almost too awful to contemplate. He told me that Dad would *never* come back home if you and he ever found out what I'd watched. He kept repeating it, driving his message home, *never, never, never*!

'I remember curling up in a tight ball, sucking my thumb, crying as Galbraith sat on the floor next to me, gently stroking my head. He ordered me to stop crying, a hard edge to his voice, saying you'd be back soon, that you'd be angry if you found out what I'd done. And then Galbraith said that we were friends, best friends, and that he wouldn't tell you if I kept the secret, too. He made me promise, actually say the words. *Friends keep secrets, Anthony*. He kept repeating it. *That's what real friends do*.'

My mother was staring at me now, as intense as I'd ever seen her, eyes unblinking, burning bright. 'Do you know, even after all of Galbraith's reassuring words, as I sat there in the park when all those awful things were happening, I knew something wasn't right. I couldn't put my finger on why, but there was a nagging, uneasy feeling I just couldn't shake off. I kept telling myself I was being ridiculous, that you'd be fine, that the doctor was there to help us, and that that was exactly what he'd do. A part of me believed it, but only a part. I tried to reassure myself, but thankfully, my doubts wouldn't go away. Something was telling me you needed me. I think it must have been a motherly instinct of some kind. I know that probably sounds ridiculous, but that's how it was.

'I started hurrying back in the direction of the clinic, walking as fast as I could, striding out, covering the distance in half the time I had on the way. I was panting hard when I tried the door handle, but the dammed thing wouldn't open. I kept trying, using all my strength, even a shoulder, to try to force it. I felt a deep sense of panic, asking myself why the hell it was locked. It didn't make any sense. I knocked hard and kept knocking, but nothing, no reply. I was getting scared by that stage. You were in there, I couldn't reach you, and that wasn't a situation I could cope with. I spotted an open window, it was small, but I decided it was just about big enough for me to climb through. I was prepared to do anything. I was that desperate.

'I prised the window open as far as it would go and somehow squeezed myself through, ripping my jeans and cutting my thigh on the latch. I think my adrenaline was pumping so very hard that I didn't feel a thing. I can remember how surprised I was when I saw the blood. But that was the last thing I was worried about. I wanted you. I found myself in a small kitchen leading to a brightly lit corridor and then the reception beyond that. I actually ran into the room, that's how worked up I felt, but I stumbled, falling, just as Galbraith entered the room with an arm around your shoulder. I could see that you'd been crying as I looked up, but oh my God, it was such a relief to see you. I can't begin to explain.'

'He'd heard you; he knew you were there,' I said. 'And he'd threatened me again, his face only inches from mine. If you ever found out what I'd done, if you ever knew I'd watched *that* film, Dad would never come home. Neither of you would ever forgive me. It would all be my fault, mine and mine alone. And I believed the bastard. I believed every dirty, lying word that came out of his filthy mouth.'

'You pulled away from him, rushing towards me, hugging me tight, not wanting to let go. But you didn't say anything, not a single word. You just stood there, clinging on.'

I formed my hands into tight fists before releasing them. The memories were all too real. 'I was terrified you'd find out I'd watched that terrible film. It kept playing in my mind, the boy, the violence, the screams, the blood. There was no way I was saying anything at all. He'd shut me right up. It was something he was good at, and he got away with his crimes for years. I was no different to many other kids. He'd shut them up too.'

'I asked him why the door was locked.'

'Yes, you did.'

'But Galbraith had an answer for everything. He explained again that it was essential that therapy sessions weren't disturbed. He reminded me that he'd made that clear at the first appointment. And I couldn't disagree with him. He had. The receptionist wasn't there, and someone could conceivably have come in and disturbed the session. I had to admit to myself that he had a point. And then he changed the focus, clever. He pointed at my bloody jeans, asking me what had happened to my leg. He insisted on cleaning the cut, applying a dressing.'

'The bastard was back in control.'

'You stood there next to me as Galbraith knelt in front of me, attending to my injury. He had me on the defensive. I felt embarrassed more than anything else. There was this doctor I'd doubted, seemingly being caring, kind and attentive. I began to think I'd made a right idiot of myself, worrying about nothing.

'He stood once he'd finished, saying it was time to arrange your next appointment. You kept asking to go home. But I just stood there like an obedient child as he flicked through the diary, searching no doubt for an early date. He said again how urgent your therapy was. And then that it would be a good idea if he saw you at his home, to give you the time you needed. You clutched my hand and started crying again, but you'd done a lot of that in recent weeks. I'd had enough of talking by that time. I agreed to the date Galbraith suggested, keen to get out of there. The hour was almost up. I hoped your father would soon arrive with the taxi. Galbraith wrote down his home address and telephone number, handing them to me before we left. He wanted me to drop you off at his house and then collect you at the end of your treatment session. It was to be a longer appointment, two whole hours.'

I gritted my teeth, my face a snarl. 'The scheming *bastard*!'

'I asked Galbraith if such a long appointment was essential. He insisted that it was, again stressing the urgency. I think I started to believe him. I began to doubt my earlier hesitation. He was the expert, so I thought he must be right. He walked us out into the car park as your father's taxi arrived, the same red one that dropped us off. You sat clutching onto me in the back seat as we drove off, heading to the main road. You rested your head on my shoulder, still not saying anything. I'd never known you so quiet. You didn't say a word. Your father asked me if you were okay, saying you seemed upset, that you'd been fine when we'd arrived. I knew he had a point; it was a good observation well made, but I decided then wasn't the time to discuss it. I thought it was something your father and I needed to talk about as adults, back at the cottage, not in the car. You kept saying you wanted to go home but nothing else. I wanted to get you there safe and sound and then talk to your dad. Even the offer of a burger couldn't tempt you. You wanted to go home. That was it. Nothing else would do.'

'It was my safe place. I needed to be in my own space. I needed my teddy.'

She patted my hand again. 'I was worried, Tony. I did care. You do understand that, don't you? I was trying to do my best. I had no idea what kind of man Galbraith was.'

'I know, Mum, honestly, I know.'

She drew her head back, straightening her back, sitting upright in her seat. 'Right, how about we take a break, have a bite to eat, and then we can talk again after lunch when we're feeling a little stronger?'

I would have preferred to continue, but I could see she was flagging. And a glass or two of red wine would be very welcome. It almost always is. 'Okay, Mum, good idea, what are we going to have?'

'How about cheese and tomato on toast with a little onion chutney? I bought some in the market last Saturday. It's home-made.'

'Mmm, yeah, that will do nicely. Now, where's that corkscrew?'

17

My mother said very little over lunch, humming along to Classic FM, directing the various orchestral performances with a waving hand rather than talk. She wasn't resistant to continuing the interview. She just needed space, and I get that. None of us is impervious to stress, and she's not as young as she once was. We started talking again at a little after two.

'You were telling me about the taxi ride home. What happened when we arrived back at the cottage?'

From my mother's face, I could see that she was back there, reliving the past as if in real time. Her voice was filled with deep feeling as she recalled events, her eyes moistening again, as they had earlier. 'You were in such a terrible state coming out of that appointment, and then again in the car, pale, clingy, tearful, complaining of a stomach ache. I sent you up to play in your bedroom while I had a private word with your father. I wouldn't say I liked doing it. I'd have much preferred to stay with you until you were feeling better. But there were important things to discuss. I had to take the opportunity while I could. He wasn't an easy man to pin down.'

I gritted my teeth. 'Galbraith *really* got to me. I was terrified that you and Dad were talking about what I'd seen. I peered under my bed and in the wardrobe to make sure Galbraith wasn't there. I *really* thought he might be hiding, hateful, ready to pounce. I reached for a favourite book, football stickers, I collected them, but I couldn't concentrate. And then you came upstairs with a hot water bottle for my stomach. I was *so* relieved when you didn't talk about what I'd seen on screen. The images were flashing behind my eyes. I couldn't get the pictures out of my head. It was Galbraith, then the boy, that poor, unfortunate boy, and then Galbraith again. I still see them sometimes all these years on.'

'I sat next to you on the bed and asked what was wrong,' said my mother. 'You were in such a good mood that morning. I asked if the doctor had upset you.'

'I said no.'

'I tried to get to the bottom of it all. I tried my best, really I did, but you kept saying that your stomach hurt. It was all I could get out of you.'

'And then you went back downstairs, and I started worrying again.'

'Your third appointment was only four days away. I told your father I was questioning the wisdom of taking you to the clinic at all. If I was going to cancel, I wanted his backing. It wasn't a decision I wanted to make alone. I needed your father to share the responsibility. I insisted he tell me what he thought: cancel or not cancel, yes or no.'

'Did he give you an answer?'

'Yes, he did, to be fair, he said to cancel, that he'd been against the idea from the start. I guess I knew that. But I needed to hear him say it. He didn't gloat; he was trying to seem supportive. And then he surprised me. It was confession time. It was so unlike him to say so much. It poured out of him. He couldn't stop once he'd started. He admitted that *all* the problems you'd experienced were down to him and he said he wanted us to get back together. He'd said similar things before, late-night phone calls when he was drunk. But this time, he seemed to mean it. I was pleased; I still loved the man despite everything he'd done. But I wasn't ready to roll out the welcome mat quite yet. I focused the conversation back on you. That was all on the Friday. I said I'd give your appointment further thought over the weekend and then ring the clinic on the Monday. Although, in truth, I'd already made the decision. You wouldn't be seeing Galbraith again.'

'Dad came upstairs to see me before he left the cottage that day. He told me he'd be moving back home soon, back for good, but not to say anything about it to you. It was our secret, my second secret of the day. Although I liked this one a lot better than the first. I'd never been so relieved. I was so glad he didn't know I'd watched that film. I'd expected him to say he'd never be coming back at all.'

She smiled thinly, slowly shaking her head. 'That was *so* like your father, always so full of himself, such a sense of entitlement. He thought he could glide through life without anything touching him. I could slap him sometimes. He rang me that evening to say he'd left Tina. He'd packed his bags and left her a note while she was out. I don't think he ever fully appreciated the seriousness of what he'd done. He expected to move right back in here with us as if he'd done nothing at all. But that was never going to happen. He hurt me. He hurt you and your sister. I wanted him back. I wanted to forgive him. But he had to earn it. In the end, he moved back in with his mother until he could prove to me that I could trust him again. And that was going to take a bit of time. It was the first step towards reconciliation. After all the shit we'd been through, I thought there were better times to come. But Galbraith had other ideas.'

'The bastard was never going to give up that easily; he was fixated on me, obsessed,' I said. 'He'd spent weeks planning, scheming, fantasising. He was always going to do all he could to get his hands on me. It's who he was. The suffering of his victims made his life worth living. The more I've learned about him, the more I've come to realise that. Such things defined him.'

Mother poured herself half a glass of wine, her first of the day. I joined her, pouring my third, filling the glass to the top.

'Galbraith didn't have it all his way. I phoned the clinic first thing on the Monday morning, the second you and Siân were on the bus for school.'

I drained half my glass, savouring the tart, zesty acidity on my tongue. I had the taste by that time. I filled my glass again, finishing the bottle. I was feeling more relaxed now, less anxious; the alcohol working its magic. 'How did that go?'

My mother spat her disdain, spittle spraying from her mouth. 'I was determined to cancel. But Galbraith was a pig of a man. He was never going to make it easy.'

She'd never said a more accurate word.

'You were undermining his plans. He must have hated that and hated you too. I bet he *loathed* you with a burning intensity. He was used to being in control. You took that from him. In his eyes, the worst thing you could have done.'

'Your bed was wet again that morning. No surprise, really, there'd been a lot of upset on the Friday. So, I wasn't in the best of moods when Sharon answered the phone. I was polite; I had no reason to upset the woman. She'd been pleasant enough to us. But I was assertive. I made it clear I wanted to cancel the appointment at Galbraith's home. And I told her that you wouldn't be seeing him again. She tried to rearrange at first, offering me an alternative date. And then when I said no, she seemed concerned, saying that Galbraith would likely want to talk to me when he returned from a conference.'

'And did he?'

'Did he what?'

'Did the bastard talk to you?'

'Oh, yes, he talked to me, all right. He rang me the very next morning. At first, he was his usual charming self, expressing his surprise, making reasoned arguments as to why the appointment should go ahead. I was reasonable, I thanked him for his input, but there was *no way* I was giving in to his pressure. He just kept on at me, and I dug my heels in even further. I was seriously annoyed by that time. There was nothing he could have said to make me change my mind. I told him again that you wouldn't be coming, not under any circumstances. And then he became *really* unpleasant.'

'Unpleasant how?'

'He demanded to know if I was a child care expert and then if your father was. He was really starting to irritate me by then. It was a side of him I hadn't encountered before. Dr Nice became Dr Nasty. And then, when that didn't work out for him, he started pleading. He kept stressing the crucial importance of you seeing him and how I was making a terrible error of judgement in cancelling. I could hear the anger in his voice, and then he sounded close to tears. It was pathetic, nauseating. I'd lost all respect for him. I put the phone down in the end. I'd had enough. I couldn't stand any more.'

'Good for you, Mum; that must have taken a lot of courage.'

She made a face. 'If only that had been the end of it!'

'But it wasn't, Mum, it wasn't. Things got so much worse from there.'

18

I'm truly delighted that both Nicola and Olivia are back home from London, Nicola having found her phone. I must admit a part of me still wonders if she really lost it at all, but I didn't challenge her. The last thing I wanted was for her to return to stay with her mother. To be honest, I'm avoiding arguments at almost any cost.

If Nicola did need a break, I could hardly blame her. I do realise I'm not an easy person to live with. I can't change my wife, but I can change myself. I'm working to achieve that end. Maybe then, if I'm successful, she won't need to go away at all. I'll be better company, more fun to be around. Nicola insisted on another one of her serious chats on the evening of her return. Once again, she waited for me to put Olivia to bed and then sat me down. She realised I was still drinking, that I'd already broken a promise I'd only made a short time before in the market café. There was an empty Irish whisky bottle in the kitchen bin that I'd been stupid enough not to hide and two new bottles in a nearby cupboard, so it wasn't difficult for her to work out. The evidence of my alcoholic excess stared her in the face. I think she was disappointed more than angry. And that was somehow worse. I'd let her down yet again, something it seems I keep doing. I say the right things, I intend to keep my promises, I'm so full of good intentions, but as she pointed out in no uncertain terms, action is more important than words. At the end of the day, when the chips are down, I never seem to come up with the goods.

Maybe I'm more like my father than I like to admit. In times of stress, the alcohol calls out to me, a temptation I find almost impossible to resist. This time has to be different if our relationship is to last. She made that crystal clear, spelling it out in unequivocal words I couldn't fail to understand.

Finally, towards the end of our discussion, I agreed to see a qualified therapist. I had hoped that wouldn't be necessary, that my writing would be enough, and maybe it will be in the long term. But for now, I accepted I needed more help. Nicola's relief was almost palpable when I eventually agreed. It's not something I'm enthusiastic about; it's a case of needs must. Anything that stinks of therapy has terrible associations for obvious reasons. But in the interests of my marriage, it's something I'm prepared to do. The quicker it's over with, the better.

* * *

I initially spoke to my GP, not in person, but on the phone, hoping for an NHS referral. But it seems such things are a lost cause. There was a waiting list of many months. Something I was happy to accept, but not Nicola. And so, I've gone private to please my wife, booking six appointments with a local consultant psychologist at £200 an hour. Whether it will be money well spent, I'm not sure. I guess only time will tell. I'll try to keep an open mind.

My first appointment is only days away. I'm counting down

the hours. I'm just glad it's a woman I'll be seeing and not a man. Any associations with Galbraith will be alleviated to some degree by her femininity. That should at least make the therapeutic process bearable. Who knows? It may even do me some good. One concern is to ensure the appointments don't get in the way of my writing. That would be a deal-breaker. I plan to make that clear to the psychologist right from the very start. Now that I've written this much, I'm determined to finish the book. This hasn't been an easy process. It's a journey with many pitfalls, and it has to mean something. It has to be read. I'm determined to triumph by the end, to destroy Galbraith's memory and send it to oblivion. That's how I'll take away his power. Then I won't need to drink. Then I will have won.

19

I've received a letter from the loathsome Gary Davies, sex offender extraordinaire, old-school, three sheets of A4, rather than another social media message as he sent before. The communication arrived on my hall floor, posted through my letterbox in a white prison envelope, handwritten in scratchy, scribbled writing, that looked as if a spider soaked in dark blue ink had wandered across the paper at will. The writing was so very bad that it took me some considerable time to decipher the letter's contents. I even resorted to using the magnifying feature on my smartphone at times to make individual words and some scrawled sentences legible.

The contents of the letter were more of the same at first, as he repeated what he'd told me with such glee and enthusiasm towards the end of my recent prison visit. And then he went on to add further detail, the nature of which I feel sure was intended to disturb and distress me for his amusement and pleasure. But if that was his intention, which I'm certain it was, it didn't work out for him nearly as well as he hoped. Because as unpleasant as reading the poisonous toad's letter was, it did at least give me a better understanding of the past. Had Davies not contacted me, there was much I would never have known.

Davies told me so much that was new to me, and I came to realise just how close he and Galbraith had been. I knew that Galbraith targeted me for weeks on end, but not the depth of his obsession or the lengths to which he went, desperate to live out his repugnant fantasies, to make them real. It's that same old pattern, fantasy followed by offending, although in Galbraith's case, it seems clear there was no remorse.

* * *

Galbraith was incensed when my mother cancelled that third appointment. Davies said the doctor told him of his hatred for her, a woman he saw as the cause of his problems. My mother had inconvenienced Galbraith, she'd got in the way, and he loathed her for that. But the doctor wasn't ready to accept defeat. The situation had become more challenging but not insurmount-able. That's the way he saw it. He was determined to overcome every obstacle, to make his fantasies real. In short, Galbraith planned to abduct me, to snatch me off the street as he had the murdered boy of a similar age, who featured in that tragic video I've previously described in such awful detail.

Galbraith wanted me imprisoned and helpless in that same windowless cellar, shackled and hanging on that same white-tiled wall. And he was willing to do anything and everything to make it happen. There were no limits to the man's depravity, and for all his intelligence, his obsessions controlled him.

Galbraith approached his plans with what he considered military precision. He took time off work, feigning illness, dedi-cating all his time and effort to his intended crimes. He borrowed an old white rusty van from a trusted sex offender contact, disguised himself in workman's clothing, overalls, a wool hat, dark glasses, and observed our family cottage day after day until finally satisfied that my father wasn't living at the property.

Galbraith looked for an opportunity to grab me, following on foot on one occasion as I walked to rugby training with a group of similarly aged friends. But I was never alone. That plan failed. And so, he watched my school at the end of each school day, finally deciding that it didn't offer a suitable snatch point either. There were too many potential witnesses. Getting caught was never a part of his plan. When all else failed, Galbraith finally decided to abduct me from our family cottage in the dead of night with the help of a suitable like-minded accomplice.

Davies claimed he served time with that unnamed accomplice, who talked of his crimes. But given the detail and enthusiasm with which Gary Davies shared the story, I feel sure that that accomplice was, in reality, *him*.

Although, like before, Davies was never going to admit to that on record. It's my firm belief that Davies wanted to tell his story, to take what he saw as the credit for his crimes, but not to pay the price.

Galbraith contacted his reluctant accomplice for the first time by phone, requiring help with a 'little plan', as he put it. The doctor had helped the man some months before, discrediting a child witness in a gross indecency case. It was time for payback.

The doctor demanded a return favour, whether the man wanted to help or not. Like the doctor's other sex offender contacts, the man feared him. He felt as if he had no choice but to do as he was told. He had no idea what Galbraith's plan entailed at that point, but he was told to buy a series of items for cash and then take them to Galbraith's address at 2 a.m. the following day. The items included a rubber torch, a glass cutting tool, and two pairs of disposable paper overalls with hoods. He was also told to wear soft-soled shoes, nothing that made even the slightest sound when walking.

* * *

The accomplice was feeling somewhat anxious when he arrived at Galbraith's large Georgian home at the appointed time. He still didn't know what the night might hold as the doctor urgently ushered him inside, checking the street for potential witnesses before finally closing the door. Galbraith asked if the man had everything required. He replied that he had, holding up a black sports bag in confirmation. Once seated at the kitchen table, Galbraith explained his criminal intentions as the man listened, becoming increasingly more anxious with each new detail. The unnamed man had no qualms about assaulting children. It was something he'd done many times before. But Galbraith's plan sounded dangerous even to someone as depraved as Davies, if it was indeed him. The chances of being caught seemed high and snatching a child could lead to a lengthy prison sentence. Galbraith became angry and abusive when the man expressed his concerns, threatening dire consequences if he failed to cooperate. That sealed the deal. There was a reptile-like coldness in the doctor's eyes as he threatened violence. Galbraith's by now very reluctant accomplice agreed to do *precisely* what he was told.

Galbraith led the man down a series of grey concrete steps and into the white-tiled cellar a few minutes later. The man was taken aback by what he saw, the hidden entrance, the steel security door, the video equipment, the implements of torture. His mind was filled with questions he was too scared to ask. He was way out of his comfort zone, inclined to run, to get out of there as fast as his feet could carry him, but instead, he stayed; he cooperated. He felt he had to.

* * *

Both men donned their overalls on Galbraith's instruction. The doctor then checked the required items before leading his accomplice back up the concrete steps, through the house, and into the cold winter street, where the same white van was waiting. Galbraith did the driving, his accomplice shivering next to him as the sleet began to fall. They travelled in almost total silence, neither saying a word until they reached the cottage. The doctor then issued his orders. The man was told to follow Galbraith's instructions without question, remaining silent until I was abducted, out of the cottage and safely secured in the back of the vehicle. That was it; the plan was that simple, except for the drug. Galbraith had a fast-acting sedative with which he intended to render me unconscious. He had a syringe and needle for that purpose, along with several glass vials of the drug stored securely in a leather pouch.

Both men were wearing surgical gloves when they entered the cottage through a ground-floor bathroom window, removing the entire double-glazed glass unit from the white plastic frame to facilitate their crime. They used the rubber torch to negotiate their way through the cottage and towards the staircase, creeping up slowly, step by cautious step, with Galbraith taking the lead. Siân was out that night staying at a friend's house, but my mother and I were asleep upstairs, each in our bedrooms, blissfully oblivious to the danger that faced us. Neither of us heard a sound as the two men crossed the landing, Galbraith opening each door in turn until he saw my sleeping form. He prepared the injection, approached my bed, pulled back my winter quilt, and in his excitement, mistakenly administered a dose of the drug far above that required to render me unconscious in seconds. I remember feeling a sudden sharp pain as he plunged the needle deep into my upper leg, but then nothing, all went black after that.

The doctor's accomplice lifted me from my bed, placed me over one shoulder, and then carried me downstairs as Galbraith watched from the landing. The man had thought that was it. He was relieved that they were about to get out of there, having achieved their goal. But Galbraith suddenly entered my mother's bedroom, where she was still asleep.

Galbraith beat my mother to a pulp that night. She's told me that she woke momentarily as he approached her, terrified as the strangely dressed intruder loomed over her. She thought she recognised him as he hit her for the first time, raising his torch high above his head, bringing it crashing down time and time again until my poor mother's face was a bloody mess of bruised flesh and fractured bone. She was unconscious long before he stopped hitting her, her skull fractured, swelling on her brain. Davies went on to say that Galbraith's face, hair and overalls were spattered in blood when he finally descended the stairs towards his trembling accomplice. The man thought Galbraith had committed murder, but thankfully, unknown to him and to Galbraith too, that wasn't the case. My mother's injuries were severe but thankfully not fatal. She clung to life.

I was carried unconscious from the cottage and thrown into the back of the van before Galbraith drove off in the direction of his home, pressing his foot down hard on the accelerator. I'm told Galbraith was as excited as a child on a Christmas morning. He couldn't wait to get his dirty hands on me. But I had to wake up first. That mattered to him above all else. That's where the pleasure was. He wanted to hear me scream. He longed to see the fear in my eyes. I was carried into Galbraith's property a short time later, still unconscious, still unaware of my fate.

Galbraith was in a jubilant mood as he shackled me to the

wall like other boys before me. But his mood suddenly darkened when he couldn't wake me. I just hung there in my chemically induced coma, lost to the world. I'd received an adult's dose of the drug, not a child's.

Galbraith slapped me repeatedly, threw several buckets of cold water in my face, and injected me with a stimulant drug, a medication intended to remedy the sedative. But, thank God, nothing worked. In the end, Galbraith used his medical skills to set up a feeding tube, something he'd done before, and it was recorded on film.

I'll be forever grateful I didn't come round. In that state, I was of no use to him. Galbraith later told Davies it was the lowest point of his life.

20

I had my first meeting with my therapist, Dr Sue Ward, a consulting psychologist with an office here in town and another in Harley Street. I suspect the London address is meant to impress, but that may be doing her a disservice. She was friendly enough, offering me a hot drink when I first arrived and welcoming me warmly. I didn't really want to be there, if I'm honest, but I tried not to let it show. If she's as expert as her qualifications suggest, maybe she worked it out for herself. It wouldn't surprise me if she did.

Our one-hour session began with me completing a tick-box questionnaire, no doubt intended to provide a benchmark assessment of my mood and behaviour, which could be revisited as the sessions proceed, measuring progress or otherwise. Dr Ward seemed reasonably confident the process would benefit me, although given I'm paying her a hefty fee, I wouldn't expect her to say anything else. I'd be delighted to be proved wrong. And, of course, I may be. It wouldn't be the first time.

We talked of my childhood, my work, my relationships, my drinking and my book. All of which she said we'd discuss in more detail as the sessions progressed. I took two chapters of the book along to the appointment with me, which she read with apparent interest, the one outlining my second appointment with Galbraith and my interview with Gary Davies. I thought letting her read the details would be easier and less stressful than telling her my story. I still tend to become tearful when discussing such things, especially if the listener shows understanding and kindness. I wanted to avoid that if I could. Whether that was wise, I'll leave it to others to judge.

As she finished reading, Dr Ward asked me if I ever experienced feelings of anger. When I said I did, she asked if I had violent thoughts. Given I'd said as much in writing, it didn't take a genius to work out that the answer was yes. She shuffled her sheaf of papers and then asked me another question as if she'd experienced some great insight. 'Thank you for sharing your manuscript with me, Anthony; it's beneficial, very informative. I'd be interested to know if you ever fantasise about hurting Galbraith, as he hurt you? Please be honest with me. Your writing suggests a repressed rage that may well be contributing to your alcohol abuse. That's something we could work to alleviate.'

I said I often indulge in such daydreams; I destroy men like Galbraith and Davies in my imaginings. They dream of hurting children, and I dream of hurting them. I don't think that's unreasonable. And I was surprised to hear that Dr Ward didn't think so either. Although she did say that she considered my dark thoughts were bordering on the obsessive. There was a potential danger in that, both for me and others. Nothing good could come from my negative thought processes.

I listened with interest, accepting she had a valid point. She suggested other ways to work through my anger, more productive methods of addressing my angst, such as talking, my writing, naturally, and meditation and physical exercise. I agreed to give it all some thought before my next one-hour session.

As I was about to leave, Dr Ward asked me one last question. I don't know if she thought she'd seen something in me or if it was a standard question in the circumstances. She asked me if I thought there was a danger I'd ever act on my violent fantasies, whether I'd ever seek to make them real as Galbraith had his. I didn't appreciate the comparison; I'm nothing like the wicked doctor and never will be. But I understood what she was getting at. The possibility I'd ever inflict actual violence on another human being wasn't something I'd really considered before, but I was quick to say no. And Dr Ward seemed satisfied with that.

* * *

As I drove away from the clinic, I wasn't nearly so sure that I'd told the truth. I remembered my father telling me of the time he assaulted Beringer. That seemed so out of character, so unlike the man I thought I knew so well. I wondered if I was any different. Do any of us truly know how we'd react when faced with extreme circumstances? I wanted to hurt Davies that day in Swansea Prison; that's the truth of it. Would I have done precisely that if it wasn't for the guard? If there were no witnesses. I don't know the answer. Part of me hopes I never find out, but only a part. That's honesty, brutal honesty; I've got issues to work through. I need more help than I realised. It seems Nicola was right all along. Maybe it's not all about the writing. There's more to me than meets the eye.

21

My final interview with my mother again took place at the cottage, but this time in the family lounge with the wood-burner in full flow, wonderfully mitigating the effects of a hard winter frost. I think Mum was glad the interview process was finally coming to an end. She didn't say as much; that's not her style. But knowing her as well as I do, her true feelings were obvious. Her body language and tone told their own story. The interview focused on the time leading up to and during the attack. I began our discussion by asking her what had happened when Galbraith and his accomplice invaded our home. She crossed her legs, rested her hands on her thighs and began talking.

'This isn't going to be an easy thing for me to talk about, Tony. I'm going to take my time. And if I need a break, you're going to have to be patient.'

'That's not a problem; I've got nothing else on this morning. We can take as long as you need.'

'And this will be the last time, yes? Tell me you're not going to ask me to repeat any of this.'

'This one final time, and we're done; that's a promise.'

'Then I'll make a start. It was a Friday. Siân was out again. I had no idea where. And you and I watched a film at about sevenish that evening. It was one of your favourites – *The Karate Kid*. We had it on video. We'd rented it so many times that the shop owner told you to keep it. I remember you were in an excellent mood. Dad was coming for a family meal the next day, and you were excited to see him. Things had been tough following your last visit to the clinic. It was good to see you with a smile on your face.'

She paused, asking if what she'd said so far was the sort of thing I was after. She continued when I confirmed that it was. I strongly suspected she was simply delaying what came next. She wiped a tear from her face.

'Are you okay, Mum?'

She ignored my question but did falteringly continue. 'I was tired. It had been a long day. We went to bed early after a mug of cocoa and some buttered toast. I read a romance book borrowed from the local library, something light-hearted, for an hour or so, and then I fell asleep. It was just like any other night. And then, and then it happened.'

'What happened? Please be as detailed as you can.'

'I must have heard something. I remember thinking I must be dreaming when I opened my eyes. It felt unreal but terrifying, totally terrifying. I could see the dark silhouette of what looked like a man slowly approaching my bed. At first, it was just a black shadow, but then the shape took on an obvious human form. I tried to move but... but it was as if I was stuck to the bed. It was as if my entire body had turned to lead. I think I was frozen in fear. That's the only thing that makes any sense. And then... and then... all of a sudden... before I could even scream, he was right there looming over me. I remember thinking I recognised his eyes before he raised his hand high above his head and hit me for the first time. *Galbraith*! It was *Galbraith*! And then, as he rained down blow after blow, all I could think about was you, the danger you were in, the risks you faced, until everything went black. The next thing I knew, it was daylight. I was in awful pain. There was... there was blood everywhere. And Siân, Siân was at my bedside trying to talk to me. I tried, I tried to ask where you were, but I couldn't speak. The words wouldn't come out of my mouth. The fear and frustration were too much to bear. I can't begin to explain how awful it was.'

I'd spent a lot of time thinking about what had happened to me back then but not so much what had happened to my mother. I was glad to listen to her story. Pleased she was able to speak about what must have been the worst time of her life.

'I'm so very sorry, Mum. This is the first time I've realised just how bad it was for you.'

My mother reached out, patting my hand, something she'd done many times before, more times than I care to count. 'I think I must have been drifting in and out of consciousness because I can remember some things but not others. It's a bit like a disjointed, interrupted film playing in my head. I see some scenes, and I miss others. I still think about it all sometimes, but not so often these days. Well, not until, not until this. The interviews have brought a lot of it back.'

'Do you remember being taken to hospital?'

She shook her head, from left to right and back again. 'Um, no, not really, I've got a vague recollection of two paramedics and a female police officer being in my bedroom at some point, but that's about it. It's like I see it all through a mist or veil. It's hazy, far from clear. My next clear memory is coming round on the ward.'

'Tell me about that.'

'Your father was there, Siân, and Bethan, the police constable.

I remember the sense of total panic when I looked around the ward and couldn't see you. It was the worst moment of my life by far, worse than the attack, infinitely worse than the physical pain. I knew Galbraith had you, I knew it to be true, but I didn't think anyone was going to believe me even if I could tell them. I'd seen the man. I recognised him just for that fraction of a moment in the half-darkness. But it still seemed crazy even to me. Why would a doctor do such a terrible thing? I thought, I thought people would think I was insane.'

She rose to her feet as I made my notes, switching on the kettle for a second time, reaching for the teabags. 'It's time for a break, Tony. We're going to have to take this slowly. The stress is getting to me. My head is starting to ache. It's not something I can talk about in one go.'

I pushed my notepad aside, switching off the recording. My mother had a point; I needed to be sensitive to her feelings. We'd finish the interview but at her pace, not mine. I smiled as she handed me my mug, her hand shaking slightly with the strain of it all.

'Okay, we're going to do this your way. This time you're in control. Tell me when you're ready to continue; there'll be no pressure from me.'

22

My sister told me of the day she discovered I was missing when I interviewed her at her workplace one cold, wet, windy lunchtime. Siân is a social worker herself these days, having qualified at Plymouth University, although she works with adults with special needs and not children. The client group was a deliberate choice. She tells me that working as a child care social worker would be too onerous a responsibility to bear after everything that happened all those years ago. There would be too many reminders of a past she hasn't come to terms with any more than I have. I'm not convinced she suffers as I do, but that's what she said. All I can do is try to accept her words at face value. I'm hoping this book helps her too.

We talked over a cup of coffee and a sandwich, sitting in her car outside her office with our coats on. In other circumstances, I would have enjoyed her company. We don't see as much of each other as I'd like these days. Not since she moved to a nearby industrial town where property prices are lower. Maybe I should make more of an effort to put our lack of contact right. And perhaps she should too. There's two of us in the relationship, and it isn't all down to me. I'm not looking forward to her finding out what I've written. But I've committed to honesty. I love her and want her to know that, but I can't protect her from the truth.

I started the interview with an open question, encouraging my sister to tell me her story in her own words. That's how I like to do things, no leading questions. I think the method gets the best results.

'Tell   me   what   happened   that   Saturday morning, *everything* you can remember, the more detail, the better.'

Siân took a sip of coffee, grimacing, saying it was too bitter, and that she preferred the blend from another café she frequented. 'I'd been out drinking the night before. I got myself in a right state, seriously pissed, and crashed out on a friend's sofa, waking up about seven the next morning. I was dreading Mum's reaction as I walked home. I hadn't said anything to her before going out, not where I was going or who with, not even how long I'd be. I'd been a right moody cow for weeks. I felt *terrible* about that afterwards when I found out what had happened to her. I felt so very guilty. I did care; it was just teenage stuff, you know what it's like; it's a developmental stage, the self-focus of youth. We all go through it.'

'You couldn't possibly have known what would happen. You don't need to explain yourself.' Those calming words have become something of a mantra in recent weeks. I'd said much the same to Mum, Dad and now to Siân too. I said it because it helped and because it was true. It sometimes seems I'm a therapist of sorts, considering others' feelings, alleviating their anxieties, conveying the right thing. If only they'd do the same for me. Mum does, of course, she's the exception, and sometimes Nicola, too, but the others, no. I think sometimes I might expect too much. Maybe seeing the psychologist isn't such a bad idea after all. I asked Siân what happened next.

'The front door was open when I got back to the cottage. I thought that was a bit strange, but it didn't worry me a great deal. I had no reason to think anything was badly wrong, not then, not yet.'

'So, when did that change? There must have been a moment, something you saw, something you heard.'

She gripped the steering wheel tightly with both hands. I could see the tension in her face as I glanced sideways. 'I couldn't hear any signs of life, so I thought maybe you and Mum must have gone out and forgotten to close the door. Either that or you were in the back garden. Although the weather wasn't great and it was still early, so that seemed unlikely. It was a relief that I seemed to have the place to myself, to be honest. I thought I was avoiding an argument. I planned to have a quick shower and then crash out in my room for a couple of hours until I felt better and could face the day. I had one hell of a hangover, a splitting headache, the taste of last night's vomit on my breath. After a quick glass of water in the kitchen, I went into the downstairs bathroom, and then I saw it. Someone had taken the glass out of the window frame. It was one hell of a shock. And there was stuff all over the floor, toothpaste, toothbrushes, make-up, a bottle of shampoo.'

'What were your initial thoughts when you witnessed the scene? What did you think had happened?'

Siân lowered her hands to her lap, shrugging, her eyes wide. I could see tears forming in her eyes as I looked in the rear-view mirror as she continued her story. 'I knew *something* wasn't right. I thought someone might have broken in. A burglary seemed the most likely explanation, but nothing seemed to be missing. Mum's purse was on the kitchen table. Her bank cards and money were still in it, I checked. And the TV was still there, the video recorder, everything. I was worried by then, starting to panic. I hurried from room to room, shouting out your and Mum's names. And then, when no one replied, I decided to look upstairs. I don't know why. I don't think I was thinking straight. If someone had broken into the cottage, they could still have been there. I guess I just needed to find you both. I wasn't such a selfish cow after all. Not when it counted, not when it really mattered.'

I swallowed the last of my shop-bought prawn and mayo sandwich. I was recording the interview but not making notes. It just wasn't practical in the car. There wasn't sufficient room for writing. 'You were brave, Siân. Be proud of yourself. You looked for Mum and me despite the dangers you faced. That's more than many would have done in the same circumstances. Did you find Mum as soon as you went upstairs?'

Siân's voice lowered almost to a whisper. 'Her bedroom door was open. I stood in the doorway. I couldn't believe what I was seeing. It was like something out of a horror film – a film I'd never want to watch. Oh my God, Tony, Mum was in such an awful state. It was *horrendous, absolutely horrendous*! My legs buckled as I approached her bed. I thought she might be dead, that I might have lost her, my mother. I puked on the carpet as I stood up. I almost ran, but I stopped myself. She needed me. If there was even the slightest chance I could help her, I had to be there. I'm glad about that now, the fact that I stayed. It makes me feel better about myself. I put her first. I wasn't selfish. I did have some redeeming qualities.'

I needed the detail, all the details, everything she remembered, however painful the memories were. 'What did you see? How bad were her injuries? For the book, I need to know the specifics.'

'I'd, er, I'd never seen anything like it, Tony. I can see her now, lying there, unable to move. She was unrecognisable as the woman I knew. Her *entire* face was a bloody mess, bruised and swollen, caked in blood, her lip torn, her nose broken, a white bone breaking the skin. And there were three of her front teeth on the carpet next to the bed. I prayed to God for the first time in years. I was ready to scream, but then I saw her breathing. That was such a *huge* relief; there was hope. I could have cheered. Her chest was moving ever so slightly, but it was moving. It wasn't wishful thinking. I knew then she was alive.'

'That must have been a good moment.' That's all I could think to say.

'Mum was trying to say something, straining, really trying her best, but no words came, just garbled sounds that made no sense at all. I put my ear close to her mouth, but it made no difference; speech was beyond her.'

I knew precisely what Siân was talking about; my mother had spoken of it too. As she lay there, battered, bruised and broken, my mother thought of me. That brought a tear to my eye; that's real love. Her concern lay with her child more than herself. 'Mum told me about that. She was trying to say my name.'

'If she'd been attacked, maybe you had too. I had the same thought.'

I wanted to know more. 'What did you do?'

'I didn't want to leave Mum alone for however short a time, the idea of it was awful. But I had to try to find you. I was terrified I'd discover you dead or badly injured like Mum was. But you weren't in your room; you weren't anywhere. But at least there was no blood. I was grateful for that. I didn't think about abduction. That possibility never crossed my mind. I thought you must be hiding somewhere, safe but too scared to come out. I looked everywhere, every room, even in the attic, but you were nowhere to be found. I hurried downstairs, grabbed the phone and dialled

999. I know I should have done that sooner, but I didn't. That's the way it was. My hands were shaking so very much that I dropped the phone. I only managed to get the number right on the third attempt. And then I went back to Mum's bedside and waited, counting the minutes, hoping help would come quickly. An ambulance came first, and then a police car a few minutes later. I could have cheered when I heard the first siren. Mum needed urgent help. I was still terrified she was going to die. And I was worried sick about you too. I'd realised you weren't hiding by then. I told myself you might be with Dad. You know, at Gran's place. But I knew that wasn't likely. It was still early. Dad slept in at weekends. And we were expecting him later in the day. Mum had invited him for a family meal.'

'Okay, I get the picture. You probably saved Mum's life.'

Siân took a paper tissue from a coat pocket, dabbing her eyes, blowing her nose. 'It's strange; it was only *after* Mum got the help she needed that the shock really hit me. I think I'd been functioning on adrenaline until then. The paramedics had arrived, they were climbing the stairs, and I was going to pieces. I was sweating, trembling, dizzy, close to passing out. But I took deep breaths, slowing my breathing, calming myself. I told myself I had to stay strong, for Mum and for you too. I stood there watching, answering what questions I could as they attended to her wounds.'

Siân drained her coffee cup before continuing. 'I was desperate to go in the ambulance with Mum, but a young policewoman who'd just turned up said she urgently needed to talk to me. Bethan Williams, I still remember her name, Bethan. She was nice enough, trying to be kind, supportive, but I didn't want to hear it. I came close to telling her to fuck off. All I wanted was to get in that ambulance before it left. But I finally agreed to cooperate when Bethan said she'd run me to South Wales General once she had the information the police needed.'

'What sort of thing did she ask you?'

'What time I went out, what time I came home, what I found. And then she bombarded me with all sorts of other questions, or that's how it felt to me, one after another. Being a witness was bad enough, I'd hate to be a suspect, question, question, fucking question. It's all pressure. Was Dad ever violent towards Mum? Had they been having a lot of arguments? Did he ever hit you or me? What was his address and contact details? Did I have a recent colour photo of you? When did I last see you? Could I give her a list of your friends, with addresses where possible? Did I have any ideas where you might be?

'It was one question after another, relentless. I answered everything as best I could. And then when I thought the questioning was finally over, two detectives turned up, a fat bloke named Inspector Gareth Gravel with an unfortunate attitude, and his sergeant, Clive Rankin, who didn't say very much at all and did what he was told. Gravel asked me *all* the same questions all over again, the exact same ones. And he wouldn't take no for an answer. He said he needed to hear it from me, in my own words, not only from the uniformed officer. She tried to tell him I'd already given her all the information they needed, but he wasn't having any of it. Maybe he didn't trust her to do her job as well as she had. He wasn't a patient man. He told her to be quiet and then focused back on me. I kept saying I wanted to contact Dad, that I needed to see him, that he'd want to know what had happened.

'But the inspector wouldn't let me ring him. And he wouldn't even give a reason that made any sense. All Gravel would say is that Bethan would let me know when seeing Dad was possible.

And he couldn't say how long that would take. That upset me. I've never felt more alone.'

'I guess they had to rule Dad out as a suspect. He might have been the attacker as far as they were concerned. They had to know.'

'Well, yeah, I realise that now. I'm not a complete numpty,' said Siân. 'But why didn't they just tell me that at the time? Maybe then I'd have understood what the hell was going on.'

'Beats me; they must have had their reasons. Maybe the detectives were focused on the crimes, finding Mum's attacker, finding me, not worrying about your feelings or anything else.'

'I needed help too, Tony. It pissed me right off then, and it still does now. At least Bethan was thinking about me. That helped. She was a nice person. I was lucky with that. She did her best.'

'What happened *after* they'd finished with their questions?'

'There's not much more to say. The detectives examined the bathroom, searched the house, and told the policewoman to take me to the hospital. Gravel told her to stay there with me and to let him know the second Mum could talk. I'd seen the state she was in, and they hadn't. I knew she wasn't going to be talking anytime soon.'

'Did you see Mum at the hospital that day, before the operation?'

'Yeah, I did. Bethan got us there quickly, as fast as she could. I think the journey must have taken about twenty minutes, certainly no longer. When we first arrived, Mum was still in casualty in a side room with a drip in her arm. She was attached to all sorts of monitoring machines, tubes everywhere. Doctors and nurses were rushing back and forth, attending to her needs as best they could. I think some of them were almost as shocked as I was. I could see it on their faces. Some tried to be nice, reassuring, saying the right things. But I could still sense their concern.

The nurse in charge told Bethan that Mum would be admitted to an acute trauma ward where she'd be assessed by a surgeon specialising in facial reconstructive surgery. I overheard the conversation, and then Bethan repeated it all to me once the nurse had walked away. I asked about contacting Dad again, but the officer said no, coming up with the same lame excuses that she didn't even seem to believe herself. I think she was struggling with it all, following orders because she had to. I kept trying to talk to Mum, and Bethan did, too, but it was a lost cause, what with the injuries and the strong painkilling drugs. They'd given Mum morphine. I heard a doctor using the word. Then a young porter covered in terrible tattoos turned up to take Mum to the ward about fifteen minutes later.'

'So, when *did you* see Dad? How long did it take?'

Siân checked her watch, pushing up her coat sleeve despite the car's dashboard clock, making it obvious. 'Is this going to take much longer, Tony? I've told you everything that matters. I've got a client at two. I can't be late.'

We had about ten minutes, according to my reckoning, maybe a little less. I was determined to finish. 'Just answer the question, and then we're done. We can talk again another time if we need to.'

My sister's tone and body language betrayed her irritation as she checked her watch for a second time. 'You mean if *you* need to. I'm not sure it's a case of *we*. This is for you, Tony, not me.'

'Please, Siân, just answer the question. We're almost finished.'

'Dad turned up with DI Gravel a couple of hours later.'

'Ah, okay, that makes sense.'

Siân started the engine, preparing to drive off, one way of bringing the interview to a close. 'I'm going to have to go, Tony, things to do, people to see. I'm a busy girl. You know how it is.'

I said one last thing as I opened the car door. 'Thanks, sis, your time's appreciated. Let me know if you think of anything else.'

She lowered the driver's side front window with an electric buzz as I stood shivering on the pavement. 'Why don't you bring Nicola and Olivia to my place for Sunday lunch? Roast beef, Yorkshire pudding, with all the trimmings. But no more book talk. Life goes on. Everyone needs a break. Let's talk about something else.'

She'd already driven off before I could think to answer. Not everyone is as keen as I am that I keep writing my story. That reality has finally dawned. Maybe Siân had a point, or perhaps she didn't. I'll give it more thought when I have the time. Galbraith impacted Siân's life as he did mine. But it wasn't *her* hanging on that white-tiled wall in that cellar full of horrors. I think it may be easier for her to move on and leave the past behind her than it is for me. If anything, my anger is rising with each chapter that passes. The depth of my feelings is intensifying. It wasn't Siân that Galbraith abducted. What is it she doesn't get about that? It was: me. Me. Me.

23

My second rugby club interview with my father was even more drunken than the first. Maybe that was necessary to encourage him to talk openly, or perhaps I'm making predictable excuses for my own alcohol excess. It wouldn't surprise me if I was. We both indulge far more than we should. But on that evening, it did at least serve a purpose. Much was said that I suspect wouldn't have been otherwise.

As we sat facing each other, lovingly cradling our glasses, my father spoke of the time he learned of my mother's attack and my disappearance, with animation. We'd both downed several pints of beer and a good few whisky chasers by the time the topics came up, loosening both his tongue and mine. Unusually for my father, he seemed keen to tell his story, using wild hand gestures to communicate his thoughts and feelings as well as his words. It was as if he was a different man. I wondered if this was the man Phillip Beringer knew, the man my father had hidden from his children all these years. The free talking individual I was now seeing with so much to say for himself. Alcohol can do that to a person; it lowers inhibitions, it loosens tongues. And on that occasion, it did precisely that, which suited me just fine. The interview went from strength to strength, so very different from what I'd expected. The more he drank, the more he talked. I'd thought it would be like getting blood from a stone.

'Do you fancy another pint, Dad?'

He lifted his glass to his mouth, making sure to swallow every last drop of the yeasty brown liquid. His words were slightly slurred. I suspect no different to my own. 'Yeah, what the hell, go on then, why not? And a packet of pork scratchings if they've got them. I'm feeling peckish.'

I handed him his order on returning to the table. 'You were telling me about the copper calling at Gran's place, DI Gareth Gravel. I'd like to know more.'

My father opened his packet, holding it out for me to take one. 'Oh, yeah, that's right, now where the hell was I?'

I refused his offer to share his meaty snack with a determined shake of my head. I hate the smell of the things and the taste even more. I can't think of anything more unpleasant. They're not for me. 'You'd just opened the front door. Why don't you go from there?'

'Ah, yeah, right, okay, I was upstairs, getting changed when the copper banged on the door, and I do mean *banged*. It was as if he was trying to break it down. The fucking thing was shaking in its frame.'

'You've already told me that. You opened the door, he held up his warrant card, and he told you he was a police officer from the West Wales Force; all very formal, all very efficient. Why don't you carry on from there?'

Dad took a mouthful of beer and nodded, swilling it around his mouth before swallowing. 'He was a right stroppy git at first, assertive; you know what I mean. And he was a big bloke, too, intimidating, a good seventeen, maybe eighteen stone, overweight but powerful-looking, big arms, big shoulders, like a rugby prop. He exuded an air of authority and looked important somehow despite a slightly dishevelled appearance. And he looked concerned. Above all, he looked concerned. I knew something was up. It had to be serious. They don't send detective inspectors if it's something trivial. I can remember my gut twisting. I thought someone might have nicked my car, something like that. As it happened, it was even worse than I feared.'

'Okay, now we're getting somewhere. What did he say to you?'

'He wasn't pissing about. He said we could either talk inside or at the police station. I didn't know what the hell to think. Arguing didn't seem like a good idea. So, I asked him in and offered him a coffee, trying to be friendly. He just started asking questions.'

'Such as?

My father began munching away at a mouthful of fried pork skin, washing it down with a generous slurp of beer as I awaited his response. He became distracted when the barmaid saun-tered past, collecting empty glasses, a tight black dress clinging to her curves. His eyes followed her as she crossed the room. He finally continued talking when I brought his attention back to the story.

'What was I saying?'

'DI Gravel was in the house, and he was asking you questions. I asked you what those questions were.'

'Oh, yeah, that's right, he, er, he wanted to know where I'd been between the hours of half-four the previous afternoon and nine-thirty that morning. He told me to be precise. To think care-fully before answering. That my reply needed to be accurate, that the timings mattered. Obviously he was trying to find out if I could have been the man the police were looking for. Although I didn't have a fucking clue what was going on at the time. I was getting more and more concerned. I told him that. I asked him what the hell was going on.'

My scribbled notes were becoming almost indecipherable by that time. I was glad to have the recording. Although there was a fair amount of background noise as the bar got gradually busier. 'Did he give you an answer?'

My father burped at full volume. 'No, he didn't, not really, not directly, anyway.'

'What's that supposed to mean?'

'He said the quicker I answered his question, the quicker he could tell me why he was there. Looking back, I don't think he ever really suspected me. I didn't have a record, no convictions for violence, nothing like that. He was doing his job, that's all, covering the bases, being a good copper. I told him I'd been in the house all afternoon the previous day, retiling the kitchen for Gran, and then I met a mate for a few pints at about half-seven that evening. Gran came into the room. She asked what was going on, and I explained. I introduced Gravel, and then she confirmed what I'd told him. Gravel asked who the mate was, where we'd been drinking, and what time I'd got back to the house. I told him I'd had a few pints with Phil here at the club and that we'd shared a taxi home about twenty to two that morning after a lock-in. Gravel didn't give a toss about the after-hours drinking. He had bigger things to worry about. As it happened, he knew Phil from work. That helped. It was easy enough for him to check out my alibi. He asked what I'd done after the taxi dropped me off. I told him I was seriously pissed. I made a quick bacon sandwich, drank a glass of water and crashed into bed until that morning when Gran woke me. He spoke to Phil on the phone, spoke to Gran again, and he was happy with that. I wasn't a suspect.'

I took a drink of lager, swaying slightly in my seat as I made my notes. 'Anything else?'

'Gravel's attitude completely changed once he knew I wasn't the man they were looking for. He sat down and gave me the bad news. Mum had been attacked at the cottage, she was at the hospital waiting for an operation, and as if that wasn't bad enough, you were missing fuck knows where. I couldn't believe what I was hearing. One minute, you're getting on with your life, doing the ordinary things people do, having a few drinks with a friend, doing a bit of tiling for your old mum, and then, *bang*, your life's blown apart. In that second, everything changes, possibly forever. I thought life might never be the same again. And I blamed myself. I should have been there. If I had been, I could have done something. Maybe your mum wouldn't have been hurt. Maybe you'd have been safe and sound tucked up in bed. It was a whole series of what-ifs that wouldn't let up.'

* * *

I could have resorted to my usual reassuring mantra as my father poured his heart out, an experience that was new to me, both surprising and informative. But I chose not to alleviate his anxiety for what I think was a good reason. I let my father wallow in his guilt because I thought he had a point. Maybe a tiny part of me still blames him, even after all this time. I know that's unreasonable; theoretically, I understand. But even with the benefit of the new understanding my writing has given me, that's still how I feel. If anything, the reflective process has reignited my resentment rather than reduced it. There's a wave of persisting anger that isn't fully resolved. It still festers somewhere deep inside me, not helping me or anyone else. Maybe that's something else to talk to the psychologist about. I'll add it to the list. I may need more than six sessions. It's getting longer by the day.

I asked my next question, something simple, just three words,

anything to move my father's story along. I wanted it told before
the alcohol obliterated my capacity for reasoned thought. 'What
happened next?'

'Gravel ran me to the hospital, asking questions on the way.'

'What sort of questions?'

My father ate one last handful of scratchings, pushing them
into his mouth with greasy fingers, emptying the packet before
throwing it aside on the table. He talked with his mouth full. 'It
was a fishing exercise, you know; he was just trying to find out
anything useful.'

I was getting frustrated with my father's lack of focus. I
thought maybe another pint would help. I waved a tenner at the
barmaid, who brought two over. I told her to keep the change.
'Oh, come on, Dad, you must remember what Gravel asked you.'

He picked up his glass. 'Yeah, yeah, of course I do.'

'Well, spit it out then.'

'Could I think of anyone with a grudge against your mum, me
or the family? Did I have any ideas where you could be? When
had I last spoken to you? That sort of thing. You know, the sort of
stuff coppers ask.'

'He was trying to build a picture.'

My father laughed, beer spilling from his mouth, running
down his chin. 'No shit, Sherlock.'

'Oh, come on, Dad, this matters to me; take it seriously.'

He was quick to answer this time, the smile disappearing
from his face. 'It was a long time ago, Tony. I can laugh now, but I
couldn't back then. Do you think I don't know what happened
was serious? I came close to collapsing when I got out of the car
in the hospital car park. Gravel took my arm and helped me; he
told me to get it together for your mum's sake. And I did; I knew it
needed saying.'

I paused for a beat, changing the subject, keen to placate

him. If I hadn't, he might have ended the interview right there and then. 'Gravel sounds like a decent man.'

'Oh, he was. Phil had known him for years. He said he was one of the best.'

'Are you okay with carrying on, Dad?'

'There are a thousand other things I'd rather be doing, but, yeah, let's get it over with.'

'Did you go straight to the ward?'

'Yeah, Cilgeran on the second floor. One of Grav's officers was waiting there with Siân. Mum was still in the operating theatre. It was a long operation. She had a lot of serious injuries. It was always going to take some time.'

He smiled and then continued. 'Siân ran towards me and hugged me tight as soon as she saw me. We were both crying. I think she stopped first. She was braver than me, probably still is.'

I didn't disagree. My father's not great in a crisis; he never was and probably never will be. It's a character flaw. He knows it, I know it. It's who he is. There was no point in pretending otherwise. After a second or two's silent contemplation, my father started talking again with a pensive expression on his face. 'I tried to find out what the hell was going on with your mother. Siân didn't know very much at all, and there was only so much the nurse in charge would tell me. So, we sat together in the dayroom, waited, and hoped for the best. Gravel was as reassuring as he could be. He said the police were doing all they could, that his best people were on the job. I think that was the best he could offer in the circumstances. He said he'd contact us immediately if there were any significant developments. He told the female constable to contact him the second your mum came round, and then he left. The surgeon who did Mum's operation came to talk to us about an hour later. A right condescending twat with a snooty south of England accent who seemed to think he was

God's gift to medicine. He stood about ten feet away from me, Siân and the copper. He couldn't even look any of us in the eye. It was as if he was looking at someone behind us when we were talking.'

I could see from my father's face that the memories were flooding back. 'What did he tell you?'

My father took a deep breath. 'It was a major procedure, high risk, which I'd already worked out for myself. It didn't take a genius. And then a total fucking shock. He said your mum had a minor cardiac event on the operating table. Those were the words the prat used, cardiac event; it was like he was talking in riddles. I asked him what the hell that was supposed to mean. I asked him a second time when he didn't answer. He finally told us that your mum had a heart attack on the operating table. She actually *died* and had to be resuscitated. Her brain was deprived of oxygen. It was touch and go for a while. It was awful, Tony. I thought I might lose her. That didn't feel good after all the shit I'd put her through. I swore if she came through, I'd never let her down again.'

I was surprised by my father's honesty. It seems drunk men tell no lies. I may have underestimated the depth of his feelings. Maybe he's a more thoughtful man than I ever appreciated, deep down where it doesn't show. He never did have another affair, or at least none I know of. Perhaps the events of that time changed him as they changed me. I hope he lived up to his promise. But I haven't asked. I might not like the answer.

'How long was it before you saw Mum?'

'She was back on the ward about two hours after the surgeon spoke to us. It seemed the operation had gone well other than, well, you know, what I've already told you. It was incredible she recovered as fast as she did. Everyone was amazed, the doctors, the nurses, everyone. I think you had a lot to do with that. She was worried; she still didn't know what had happened to you. She was one determined woman. If there was anything she could do to make sure you were okay, she was going to do it. She's stronger than me, mentally, I mean, not physically. She was never going to give up. That's the sort of woman she is.'

I made my final scribbled notes before closing my notepad and putting it back in my briefcase for safekeeping until the next time it was needed. I was pleased with how the interview had gone as I switched off the recording, more glad than expected, even in my slightly dizzy alcoholic haze.

* * *

I decided to stay at my parents' cottage that night rather than go home to my wife and child. I slept in a spare room at the back of the cottage, once my childhood bedroom. The same room from which the two predators had taken me thirty years before. It still looks much the same as it did back then, the same yellow curtains, the same multi-coloured floral carpet, a little worn in places, much like myself. It was almost as if I was a child again. As if the passing years had melted away.

I phoned Nicola before finally slumping into bed, telling her that Dad and I had talked late into the evening and that my car was playing up. I said I'd get it sorted in the morning when garages were open. In reality, I didn't want her to see me drunk. I'd let her down yet again, despite all of my well-intentioned promises. It might well have been the last straw if she'd seen the state I was in. It wasn't a pretty sight. Whether she believed me, who knows? But she didn't say anything to the contrary when I saw her the next day. Although she did ask me the date of my next appointment with the psychologist. I can be incredibly foolish sometimes for a supposedly intelligent man with an above-average IQ. I suspect her question meant she saw through me all along. Nicola knows me only too well. She can read me like a large-print book.

And so, it seems my father isn't the only one with shortcomings. None of us is perfect. We all have our flaws. Perhaps I shouldn't be so quick to judge. It's easier to recognise the failings of others than our own.

I bought Nicola a bunch of twelve red roses and a large box of dark chocolates, her favourites. She's put up with a great deal from me lately, of that I'm acutely aware. It seems another grovelling apology is in the offing. There's been far too many of those in recent weeks. I hope and pray she accepts this one with good grace as she has all the others. And I hope this time my well-intentioned words of regret mean something, that I act on them, that I think about them when the demon drink next tempts me. It's action that counts. Apologies are words, nothing more. If I don't stop drinking, what use is one more? I know the truth, the reality, it's of no use at all.

24

I finally tracked down former Police Constable Bethan Williams with the help of Detective Sergeant Pam Forsyth, who contacted her ex-colleague on my behalf. Bethan, as she told me to call her, 'no need for formalities', rang me on my mobile two days later. I was beginning to think she wouldn't call and was glad to hear from her. She spoke with a Welsh musical accent I was entirely familiar with, although I think her voice is significantly more distinct than mine.

Bethan told me she'd taken retirement from the force two years before and was now running a small café in a coastal village a few miles from Tenby on the Pembrokeshire coast. She was initially reluctant to agree to an interview in person, preferring to talk on the phone. But when I mentioned my sister and mother by name, Bethan had a welcome change of heart. She even went as far as to say that my mother was one of the most remarkable women she'd ever met. That was nice to hear, but to be honest, it surprised me. I hadn't thought of my mother in that way before. However, I understood days later when the ex-officer told me more. My mother's actions were indeed remarkable. I now think that word is entirely apt.

The interview was arranged at Bethan's seaside café the following evening at six, half an hour after the premises was due to close. She told me she wanted time to prepare before I got there. It seemed an entirely reasonable request, one with which I was happy to comply. I was glad our meeting was happening at all.

I drove the thirty or so miles from my hometown to the café with a favourite classical music compilation playing on the car stereo, one soaring female operatic aria after another raising my spirits despite the winter chill. I knew Pembrokeshire reasonably well, having travelled to various bucket-and-spade beaches with my family in the warmer summer months. But I didn't know Bethan's particular village, relying on the car's sat nav to get me there.

* * *

I found the brightly lit café with relative ease, parked my hatchback, and hurried towards the entrance, acutely aware that I was a few minutes late. There was a closed sign on the door, but it was unlocked, enabling me to walk in to be met by Bethan Williams, a grey-haired woman of average build, dressed casually in blue jeans and a thick, brightly coloured jumper. She was wearing large hooped earrings and had bright red lipstick that stood out against her pale features. I would never have guessed she was an ex-police officer had I not known of her background. Maybe she likes it that way, or maybe not. I have no way of knowing.

She warmly welcomed me with the offer of coffee which I was pleased to accept. We sat down at a table close to the door. She didn't have a hot drink herself. I think she was keen to get down to business. As soon as we sat down, she simply asked me what I wanted to know. I took out my notepad, happy to get on with the interview. It suited her, and it worked for me. I chose not to record the interview. I'm not sure why.

'You were there at the cottage that morning when my sister found my mother?'

She nodded twice. 'Yes, I was. I was driving the panda car that day, on a six till two shift. I got a call over the car radio saying a woman had been attacked. I didn't know you were missing until I reached the cottage.'

I looked back at her with a puzzled expression. 'I thought my sister had told the call handler when she dialled 999.'

'She had, but for whatever reason, that information didn't get to me. Not until your sister told me herself.'

I wondered if Bethan was misremembering after so many years. But there seemed little, if any, point in challenging her. Either way, it didn't change the story significantly. What would be the point? I might have interrupted her flow.

'I've talked to my sister at length about what happened that morning. I think I know the detail. I don't know if there's anything *particular* you'd like to say before we move on to talk about what happened at the hospital? I'll leave it to you to judge.'

Bethan told me much the same as Siân had, summarising events quickly and succinctly, stressing the severity of what she described as my mother's 'shocking injuries'. She also talked of Siân's stoic courage and determination. She, like Siân, had feared my mother might die. From what I understand, she very nearly did. I listened with interest to what Bethan had to tell me, although nothing new she chose to share struck me as being of any particular significance until she focused on the hospital.

Then everything changed. Events related to my disappearance were far more dramatic than I'd ever realised.

* * *

'I waited with Siân at the hospital, keeping her company along with your father while the doctors did their job. DI Gravel had told me to stay there. He was heading up the investigation into your abduction. Finding you, hopefully finding you alive, was his number one priority. And he wanted everything done quickly. The chances of finding a missing child alive reduce with every hour that passes. He was hoping your mother had information that could help us find you. Maybe she'd seen her attacker? Maybe she could describe him? I was to talk to her the second an interview was possible and keep DI Gravel notified of all develop-ments, whatever the time of night or day. Your mother had a major operation; as I said, her injuries were awful, we weren't confident we'd be able to interview her at all. But she surprised the doctors and us too. Your mother was one determined lady.'

I was genuinely interested by that stage of the interview, keen to know more. 'Can you expand on that for me?'

'She was drifting in and out of consciousness for several hours after the operation as the anaesthetic gradually wore off. She was back in the ward after a period in recovery, with me, Siân, and your father taking turns to sit at her bedside. Both Siân and your father were under strict instructions to notify me imme-diately if your mother said anything. I think your mother was at least partially aware of her surroundings by that stage. She'd blinked open her eyes once or twice before quickly drifting back to sleep. I could see her confusion, her fear; it was written all over her face. But for then, communication seemed beyond her.

'She later told me that she was unsure if the terrifying

pictures in her head were memories or nightmares. Something she was desperate to clarify when she eventually came round. Hugely frustratingly, I'd popped to the toilet when she did finally open her eyes. Siân rushed to get me. She told me your mother had struggled desperately to speak, looking your father in the eye and uttering one word, ever so slowly, ever so quietly. It was garbled, difficult to understand, but she'd said your name, 'Anthony'. Your mother's eyes flitted around the ward, and I've no doubt she was looking for you. And I think your father knew that too. But he couldn't bear to tell her what had happened. He thought the information would be too hard for her to cope with, that the burden would be too much.

'That's all assumption, but I'm sure I'm probably correct. He'd already left your mother's bedside by the time I got there. I saw him rushing away down a corridor in the direction of the exit. Siân told me he'd told your mother to concentrate on getting well before he left. He avoided a difficult conversation, and I get that, not everyone can handle that degree of stress. But it was a luxury I couldn't afford. I had a job to do. I had to get on with it.'

I thought the situation described by the officer typical of my father. Maybe, if I'm generous, I could argue he felt he was doing the right thing, but if I'm honest with myself, which I must be, I suspect he was thinking more of himself.

'Were you able to talk to my mother? Did she say anything more?'

The former officer shifted in her seat, her eyes narrowed, focused on me as she provided her answer. She had so much more to say.

'The poor woman was weeping pitifully when I reached her bedside. There was a look of complete panic on her bruised and battered face. She wanted the truth, and she *needed* the truth. She somehow managed to say that one word, slowly as if she was spelling it out, 't-r-u-th'. Siân was still there with me, being strong, selfless, holding your mother's hand. I can remember Siân looking me in the eye, imploring me to speak, such a brave girl. And I did; I told your mother everything. I had to for her sake and the sake of the case too. I told her who I was, why I was there, and everything that had happened. I told her that she'd been attacked while she lay in bed in the cottage, that she'd had an operation to attend to her many injuries. Your mother desperately tried to speak, but she was exhausted. Her mouth was swelling with the effort of it all, and blood was seeping from her stitches. All I could hear was mumbled, distorted, incomprehensible sounds, more white noise than language. I asked Siân for clarification, more in hope than expectation, but she hadn't understood anything either.

'I knew if I were to gain any useful evidence, I had to be imaginative in my methods. I thought maybe if your mother couldn't speak, she could write. I wasn't sure if my idea had any chance of success, but it had to be worth a try. You were missing, highly likely in the hands of a vicious predator, either alive or dead. There was everything to gain and nothing to lose. I hurried from the ward to a small voluntary run shop on the floor below, returning as quickly as I could with a notepad and a large black felt marker pen; I thought it might be easier for your mother to hold. I held both items up in front of her, asking if she thought she could write. I was delighted when she nodded. I helped prop her up in a reclined seated position supported by several pillows. She rested the pad on the palm of one hand, holding the pen in the other. I can remember her hand shaking wildly as she wrote her first sentence in bold capitals. "WHERE IS ANTHONY?"'

Bethan paused before continuing, thoughtful, reflective, as I waited, my pen poised. 'I've got to be honest. I was close to tears when I gave her the answer. I was just about holding it together.

There was no easy way of saying it, no way of softening the blow. So, I told your mother *exactly* how it was, holding nothing back. I told her that you were missing, that we were searching for you, but hadn't found you. If she knew the full facts, she might have been able to help. And she did. I asked her if she'd seen anything, heard anything, anything that could help us when the intruder was in the house. And she wrote with urgency, in bold capitals again, turning the notebook on its side, filling an entire new blank page. "DR DAVID GALBRAITH!"'

'She wrote his name?'

'Yes, yes, she did.'

'How did you react?'

'Well, it wasn't exactly what I was expecting. I thought she was confused. She hadn't long had a major operation, and there were still a lot of drugs in her system. I knew Galbraith. I'd been at a child protection case conference with him. And I knew nothing of the organised abuse investigation, not then. The idea of Galbraith being the predatory criminal we were looking for seemed highly unlikely to me. But I tried to keep an open mind. I asked her if she was saying Galbraith had attacked her. I needed to be sure. She wrote one word, "YES". I responded by telling your mother I'd contact the officer in charge of the case immediately to share what she'd told me. She wrote one last thing. "FIND MY SON!"'

I could feel my eyes fill with tears. 'Wow, I er, I get what you said on the phone, remarkable indeed.'

'She's quite the hero.'

'Yeah, absolutely, I had no idea.'

'With hindsight, I'm certain Galbraith thought he'd killed her. DI Gravel thought the same. Galbraith wasn't expecting your mother to give his name to me or anybody else.'

'It's the only thing that makes any sense.'

Bethan folded her arms across her chest. 'Are we done?'

'I'd like to know how Gareth Gravel reacted to your call.'

'Another coffee?'

I said yes, and this time she joined me.

* * *

'I was feeling slightly nervous when I rang Grav, butterflies in my stomach. I thought he was going to tell me I was being ridiculous and chastise me for wasting his time. He wasn't always an easy man to deal with; he didn't suffer fools gladly. But it wasn't like that. He didn't seem surprised at all. And then everything happened quickly, multiple arrests, kids being taken into care. I wasn't a part of that, but it became common knowledge in the force. There's only so long you can keep something like that secret once the shit hits the fan. You'd better speak to someone else about all that, DI Simpson maybe. I think I've told you everything I can.'

I thanked her, both for giving the interview and for the significant part she'd played in helping my seven-year-old self.

She lifted an open hand to the side of her head in mock salute, lightening the mood. 'All part of the job. Glad to be of service.'

'Would you like a copy of the book if it's ever published?'

'Yes, why not? That would be great. Please put it in the post and sign it too. And give my best wishes to your mother and sister. Tell them to say hello if they're ever down this way.'

I said that I would before walking away. I fully intend to keep my promise. I owe Bethan Williams a debt of gratitude. It's the very least I can do.

25

I wasn't able to interview ex-Detective Inspector Trevor Simpson as I'd hoped. He lives in a villa on the north coast of Tenerife these days, having retired from the force several years ago. Simpson didn't respond to my first two social media messages, but he did to my third. He was polite, courteous, but firm, leaving no room for ambiguity. In short, he wants no part of the book. He didn't explain why, and I didn't ask. He said never to contact him again, an instruction I'll respect.

Neither was I able to interview DI Gareth Gravel, the officer so liked and respected by my father. A further interview with Phillip Beringer wasn't possible either, due to the nature of the first. I'm sure I don't need to explain. Therefore, I was reliant on Mel Nicholson to discuss further the progress of the joint police and social work investigation, and the flurry of coordinated action that followed. He'd been an active, if non-operational, part of the process at every stage. I would have liked to interview the supervising police officers and Beringer, too, given the operational nature of their roles. But as none of that was possible, Nicholson provided a welcome and acceptable second best.

My next meeting with Nicholson again took place at his comfortable home. But this time, we sat in a pleasant sunlit conservatory at the back of his detached property with an uninterrupted view of a lawned garden bordered by evergreen trees and shrubs providing shelter and privacy. There'd been a light dusting of snow the previous day, followed by a hard night-time frost. But a freestanding gas cylinder heater with a beaten copper front provided ample warmth as the two of us sat talking over cups of aromatic percolated coffee and milk chocolate digestive biscuits.

* * *

Nicholson answered my questions with patience and care. Once again, I was grateful to him for his willing cooperation. He's contributed a good deal to this book. It couldn't have been written without him. I'm also grateful to his wife for making me as welcome as she did. She didn't have to do that, and it's appreciated.

Nicholson became increasingly reflective as he spoke to me that day, the enormity of events still engendering a strong emotional reaction even after thirty years. That's not an assumption on my part; I asked him if my observation was correct, and he confirmed it was. The memories are still as real for him as they are for me. This is what he said.

'Living with the knowledge that children were likely being abused while the investigation was ongoing was truly awful. Children were at risk; we knew that with 100 per cent certainty. I can't begin to explain how hard that reality was to deal with. But we had to gather evidence. There was no other choice. And the investigation lasted weeks, not days, *weeks*! I was losing sleep, struggling to eat, thinking of little else. And I wasn't alone.

Everyone involved was desperate to act. Phillip Beringer was putting more and more pressure on me, making phone call after phone call, as if I could somehow magically conjure up the necessary additional evidence to enable us to act. Trevor Simpson made repeated calls to the Crown Prosecution Service, presenting evidence, making a case for charges, but the lawyers always wanted more. And then your mother named Galbraith as her attacker, and it all came to a head. It was a pivotal moment. Everything else stemmed from that.'

I interrupted him in full flow. 'I've spoken to the policewoman to whom Mum made her disclosures, Bethan, Bethan Williams. It was clever of her to ask my mother to write things down. And then she took my mother's allegations seriously. Not everybody would have done that. They must have sounded crazy. But thank God she did. She said things moved very quickly after that.'

Nicholson bent at the waist, leaning towards me. He adjusted his plastic-framed glasses, using a finger to push them to the top of his nose. 'Yes, they did, and that was a *huge* relief. The information your mother provided was a complete game-changer. I don't think her evidence would necessarily have resulted in immediate action in itself, particularly given the context. She was describing an attacker she'd only seen briefly in the semi-darkness, she'd suffered serious head injuries, and she was on a great deal of medication. She could hardly have been considered the most reliable of witnesses given the state she was in. Any half-decent barrister would have torn her evidence to pieces. But when seen in the light of the video evidence already obtained against Galbraith from the various child witnesses, what your mother told PC Williams was compelling. And you, a seven-year-old boy, were still missing. There was every chance Galbraith *had* abducted you, quite possibly that he still had you imprisoned somewhere, just as your mother suspected. We knew

Galbraith was capable of serious violence. If you were alive, your life was in danger. It doesn't get any more serious than that.

'So, we acted quickly. I met with Trevor Simpson and Phillip Beringer at police headquarters to put a proposed action plan together. The top brass approved it that same day, and then the CPS gave it the final go-ahead about an hour later, after a bit of pressure from the chief constable. Then it was a case of urgently getting everyone together from the various agencies involved to update them on events and ensure they all knew their responsibilities. I chaired that meeting at the children's resource centre later that same day.'

As I listened to Nicholson with interest, I was hungry despite a residual hangover that wouldn't let up. I dunked a biscuit in my coffee, thinking the sugar might do me some good. But all it did was make me feel sick. I focused back on the interview. 'How had the investigation gone?'

'Pretty well, all considered. It was far from perfect, but it could have been one hell of a lot worse. We had the key players well in the frame by that stage. There were still far too many offenders we didn't have enough on to arrest and others who hadn't even been identified, but we'd delayed long enough. We had to pull in those we could. And the evidence we did have seemed indisputable, that against Galbraith included.'

'Anything specific?'

'The police already had more than enough to charge him. Galbraith was even more involved with the ring than we'd realised. Several children had described him committing a series of serious sexual offences. Not that any sexual offence isn't serious. It's just that some carry a longer potential prison sentence than others. Galbraith's depravity knew no bounds. I won't go into the details. You don't need me to tell you the kind of horrors he was capable of. Trevor called him evil, and I can't say I disagreed with him. Many labels come to mind, monster, beast, animal, nonce, but I think Trevor judged it just about right. We were desperate to put the bastard away, and the other offenders too. The safety of a lot of children was on the line. The investigative teams did a tremendous job gathering evidence. It can't have been easy to gain the children's trust after all they'd been through. And now it was our turn. And that was a lot of pressure. We knew we had to get everything exactly right, everything by the book, no mistakes.

'There was so much at stake, and there was always the potential for things to go horribly wrong. We were all hugely relieved it was all finally happening, but that didn't stop us worrying.'

My headache was finally subsiding. Nicholson had my undivided attention, and I was gripped. I needed to know more. 'What happened at the meeting?'

'I went through the motions, welcoming the attendees, facilitating introductions, explaining the purpose of the gathering, that sort of thing. It was all completely unnecessary, to be honest. Everyone knew each other and why we were there. I think it was a comfort blanket of sorts, a familiar ritual that settled my nerves. And then, once the formalities were out of the way, I asked Trevor Simpson to outline *exactly* what we were dealing with. I didn't want anyone to underestimate how big a job was ahead of us. I knew Trevor was the best person to put everyone in the picture. Although I'm sure Phil could have done just as good a job of it.'

I turned to the next page of my notebook, preparing to continue writing. I made a silent commitment to learning shorthand as my hand began to ache. It sometimes does in the colder months. 'What did Simpson say?'

'He summarised everything we knew succinctly and professionally. He talked about the unprecedented size of the ring, both perpetrators and victims, and then about the heinous nature of the many offences committed. From what we could tell, it had all been going on for years. Some of the alleged abusers were already known to us, but very few had been successfully prosecuted up to that point. Hopefully, that was about to change. Trevor kept stressing the scale and seriousness of the investigation, and he did a brilliant job. When he asked if anyone had any questions, nobody said a word. I think those not directly involved in the day-to-day investigative process were stunned. It wasn't like anything any of us had ever had to face before. And thank God we never did again.'

I was glad of the information, but I needed more. I wanted as complete a picture as possible. Nothing less was acceptable. 'So, okay, Simpson provided a summary, setting the scene, I get that. But what happened next?'

'He asked Phillip Beringer to outline the agreed plan of action, which is exactly what he did. Although he didn't stand as Trevor had, it wasn't Phil's style. I think he was trying to seem a lot more relaxed than he felt. I can't blame him. I was doing the same thing.'

'I'm very interested to know what was agreed.'

Nicholson raised his cup to his mouth, drinking what was left of his coffee. For the first time, there was a hint of impatience in his tone. I think he was irritated by my rush to get his story told.

'Yes, I was just coming to that. Like I said, we had no choice but to focus on those offenders we had a reasonable chance of convicting. It would have been nice to get all of them, but that was never going to happen. Not with the system we were working with. It was all about what we could prove. The CPS had sanctioned five arrests, four men and one woman, and two further arrests, both men, looked likely depending on additional evidence to be gathered in video interviews that same afternoon. All the agreed suspects would be simultaneously arrested by teams of two detectives accompanied by uniformed officers. The arrests would take place early the following morning, providing an element of surprise.

'The suspects' children would then be interviewed at one of the county's two video interview facilities by child protection police officers and social workers, following which they'd be medically examined by one of two experienced consultant paediatricians. All the children would be screened for sexually transmitted diseases, including HIV. One of the suspects was known to be positive. A team of social services resource centre workers would transport the children from their homes to the interview suites and for medicals as needed. Suitable foster placements were ready and waiting when required.

'DI Gravel and DS Rankin were given the job of arresting Galbraith. His house would be thoroughly searched at the time of his arrest. Your father had given the police an item of your clothing, a jumper, I think, but I can't be sure, to help facilitate the search. A sniffer dog would be given the scent. The police hoped the dog would take them straight to you.

'Although, of course, you may not have been at Galbraith's home at all. We didn't know where you were. You could have been anywhere. We couldn't go searching Galbraith's place right there and then, however tempting. It's like I said, all suspects had to be arrested at the same time, early, when we knew where they were, at home in their beds. One last waiting game that was hard to take. But at least then, action was only hours away. It was all finally coming to a head.

'We'd tried to cover all the angles, dot the Is, cross the Ts, to think of every possible circumstance where something could potentially go wrong. But there were still so many imponderables. There always are when people are involved. One way or another, it was going to be a momentous day.'

* * *

I thanked Mel Nicholson again for his willing cooperation, placed
my notepad back in my briefcase, stood and shook his hand. That
was the last time I saw him, and I don't expect to see him again. I
hope he has a happy retirement and that his writing goes from
strength to strength. From what I can tell, he's dealt with the past
so much better than I have. My scars seem more profound.
Galbraith has more of a hold on me than he does on him. I hope
to loosen the doctor's grip before I bring this book to an end.
Whether I succeed is a matter of conjecture.

26

I've had my second appointment with Dr Sue Ward, the eminent local psychologist. I have to admit it wasn't the most productive hour I've ever spent. And that, I'm afraid, was almost entirely down to me. The more I've learnt of the events of thirty years ago, the more enraged I've become by the thought of Gary Davies's impending release. Dr Ward wanted to talk about so much more, my relationship with Nicola, my role as a father, my work as a journalist, and of course, this book. But my thoughts and words kept returning to Davies, my deep sense of injustice burning bright almost to the point of obsession.

She asked if I'd tried the meditation she recommended as a stress-relieving remedy, but I had to admit the answer was an emphatic no. I just can't find the time, and if I'm to be honest, as I must be, I find the lure of alcohol a far more attractive proposition than some new-age contemplation, which I doubt would achieve very much at all. The very idea that Davies will soon be back on the streets, very likely in my town, makes me boil with rage. I'm seriously considering making his release public knowledge. I've thought of social media and maybe even printed posters warning parents of the dangers posed to their children. Neither Dr Ward nor Nicola thought it a good idea, but it seems eminently sensible to me.

* * *

Sadly, Nicola and Olivia were back in London, back with my mother-in-law but for longer this time. I didn't stop drinking as I promised I would. My words of regret and good intention came to nothing, as I feared they might. She pleaded and pleaded again, 'stop drinking, Tony, please stop', but even that wasn't enough. I couldn't blame her for going, I did understand she needed the break, but that didn't make it any easier on me. I can't pretend I was anything other than disappointed, although that is perhaps understating the case. I was crushed. I think that's more accurate. But I decided not to make the journey myself this time. It seemed sensible to give Nicola the space she so clearly craved. I told myself she'd return when she was good and ready, or at least that's the hypothesis I clung on to, and then we'd try again.

It was my dear Olivia I missed the most, the bedtime stories, the affectionate hugs, the smile on her pretty face when she greeted me, although even the thought of potentially losing my lovely daughter wasn't enough to stop me from resorting to the demon drink. That's not an easy thing for me to admit. It doesn't make me feel good about myself.

* * *

They are back home with me now after an eight-night trip, a positive, at least they came back, but my relationship with Nicola remains strained almost to the point of breaking. Our brief honeymoon period before my return to Wales during her last

London visit now seems so long ago, although, in reality, only a short time has passed. I'm still very much hoping the writing process makes a positive difference, but with each chapter that passes, a part of me fears that certain aspects of my story are just too painful to face without negative consequences. But having said all that, there is always hope, even in the darkest of times. I tell myself the white light of hope still shines somewhere in the distance. And that spark of optimism stems from an unexpected place.

In the following two chapters, I'm going to tell you more about Cynthia, a story I've found both inspirational and moving. I find myself echoing my father's words. I think Cynthia is stronger than me and braver too. I hope I can find even a small part of her strength. Maybe then I'll triumph; I'll rise like a phoenix from the ashes. Perhaps then memories of David Galbraith and his like-minded kind will be destroyed forever. I can only hope that's the case, for me, for Nicola and for Olivia too.

27

Cynthia told me of the day of Galbraith's arrest as we sat together in that same pleasant vegetarian Merlin's Lane café for a second interview. Although we positioned ourselves on a comfortable black leather settee close to the serving counter this time, rather than at a table as we had before. I remember a framed charcoal drawing of a breastfeeding mother on the wall opposite the sofa and a small bookcase rammed with all kinds of books and periodicals to our immediate right. Low-level relaxing music was playing on the sound system as customers came and went, ordinary life going on all around us as we talked of events that were far from mundane.

Cynthia told me that things moved very rapidly during what was a highly turbulent period of her life. It's clear from what she said to me that she was still very much under Galbraith's cunning, dishonest, and unscrupulous spell that early morning when the police banged on her door. Even watching my father appealing for information on the Welsh evening news hadn't been enough to shake off her husband's controlling influence. This is what she told me, her story in her own words. It explains a lot about her and a good idea more about the depraved doctor too.

'I'd been up from bed for an hour or so, preparing David's breakfast, checking and rechecking that everything was right, everything in its correct place and at the correct distance. It was always a stressful time, watching the clock, listening for any sound of movement from the first floor, anticipating the inevitable inspection and criticisms when he finally appeared. And then, at half-past six that morning, there was a knock on the door that made me jump. I was hyper-vigilant in those days, always on full alert. I was close to panicking as the knocking got louder. Not because of who it might be or what they may want, but because David might be woken before his usual time. He wasn't due to get up for another hour. I knew I'd get the blame for the disturbance, and blame meant punishment. He saw anything that went wrong as my fault.

'I rushed for the door, hoping to stop the noise, stumbling and falling in the hall before getting back to my feet and reaching for the handle. Even when I saw the police standing there, my first thought was of David's reaction. I didn't even ask myself why they were there. I just wanted quiet. I wanted them gone. Five officers crowded around the entrance: three uniformed constables – two women and one man – one with a dog, and two male detectives, one of whom I recognised from the television appeal. He'd been sitting next to your father.'

'DI Gravel?' I said.

'Yes, that's right, he, er, he stood in the doorway, obviously in charge. He confirmed who I was and then demanded to know where David was. And I do mean *demanded*. But even then, all I could think of was the early hour, what David would think, how angry he'd be if woken prematurely, and what form of punishment he'd inflict. I just stood there blocking the door, not thinking for one minute that they might be there for a good reason or that they had a job to do. I didn't see them as potential saviours but as a threat. That seems crazy to me now, but it's how it was.' Cynthia laughed despite herself, a cold laugh that was anything but comic. 'I told Gravel he'd have to make an appointment. Can you imagine that? Five police officers were standing there in front of me, and all I could think about was not disturbing my husband before he was ready for breakfast. I really was that obsessed with meeting his expectations. I even tried to close the door. I tried to slam it shut. I was far more afraid of David than of the police.'

'What happened?'

'Gravel put his foot in the door, and then his sergeant, DS Rankin, shoved it open. They all crowded in as I fell backwards, Gravel taking the lead. And then he helped me to my feet. He asked again where David was and said they'd search the house if I didn't tell him. I finally began asking myself if the police being there could have something to do with the boy I'd seen being carried into the house late one night as I watched, from my bedroom window, but pleasing David still seemed far more important. My mind was racing, faster and faster, one conflicted thought after another.'

I jerked my head back. 'Hang on, let's go back a bit, are you saying you saw me being carried into the house and did *nothing*?'

Cynthia lowered her eyes, looking at the low table in front of her rather than me. 'Look, Tony, I know my explanation is going to sound pathetically inadequate, but I was completely controlled by the man. I was in total denial. Yes, I did see you, I know it was you, I remember your red hair. But I told myself that you must have been in an accident, that my husband was a doctor, and that you'd receive the help you needed. I know that must sound crazy, and I'm so very sorry I didn't do something right there and then.

But I was beaten down, broken, lying to myself as a means of self-protection. I couldn't face the truth then, not yet, it was far too painful, too brutal, and so I returned to bed, burying my head under the pillow, silencing my thoughts, hiding from the world, listening as the Welsh dresser was pushed aside in the kitchen. I so regret that now, my actions in the interests of survival. But it wouldn't always be that way. And I did tell the police where David was that morning they came to the house. At least I did that.'

Cynthia's words, body language and pained expressions told their own story. I got the distinct impression she was racked with guilt. And for me, at that stage of the interview, that was enough. 'Okay, I understand, let's get back to the story. The police had just forced their way into your house.'

She looked relieved, almost younger, as if a weight had lifted from her. But her expression darkened again as she began talking. 'Yes, yes, that's right. The police were all crowded in the hall. And Gravel was demanding to know where David was. I was still trying to figure out what on earth to do for the best when my two lovely girls appeared at the top of the stairs. They were crying silent tears, both of them not making a sound. It was something they'd learnt, something they were good at. They didn't want to disturb their father any more than I did. It pained me to see them like that, and in an instant, I knew I had to prioritise their needs. Whatever David said, whatever punishment he chose to inflict on me, my girls finally had to come first.

'David had slept in his study the night before. It was something he did often. As I climbed the stairs, I told Gravel where he was. My entire body was shaking as I brought Elizabeth and Sarah downstairs, where we were ordered to wait in a sitting room to the side of the hall in the company of a policewoman named Pam. I sat there, trying to comfort my girls, to say the right things, asking myself what the hell was going on and how angry

David's reaction would be. Although, in my heart knowing that something much worse was at stake. I was filled with anxiety when Gravel told Pam to stay with us until someone arrived from the social services. David had often said I was an inadequate mother. That one day, the social workers would come to take my girls away. Now it seemed David had been correct all along. My worst nightmares seemed to be coming true.

'I can still remember the confused look on Pam's face when I began pleading with her not to take my girls away. She was kind, reassuring, saying all the right things, but I thought it was all an act intended to deceive me. Time and again, David had warned me never to trust the authorities. That their seemingly good intentions would be a cunning ploy to catch me out. His cautionary lies echoed in my head as I sat there.

'I can see now that all he was doing was trying to silence me, to control me. To stop me from saying anything that might implicate him in any crimes. But I didn't see it then. I decided to say nothing at all. His strategy worked only too well. Stay tight-lipped; that was best.'

'What happened next?'

A quickly vanishing smile flashed on Cynthia's face as she continued telling her story. 'There was a lot of noise, shouting, banging and swearing. And then I saw Gravel shoving David down the hall past the open door of the room we were in with such force that he struggled to keep his footing. I can't begin to explain how shocked I was. I couldn't believe that anyone would dare treat my husband in such a way. And the look of disbelief on David's face – the rage. I stood and watched in amazement as he was shoved out into the street and thrown into the back of a police car. A uniformed officer followed, carrying David's computer equipment while the others searched the house with the dog. Pam told me to sit back down and wait until someone arrived from social services.'

'Did you tell the police about the cellar?'

Cynthia lowered her gaze again, refocusing on the tabletop as before, avoiding my eyes. I could sense her regret before she opened her mouth to speak. 'No, I'm sorry, I didn't say a word. I knew you were down there, but I couldn't bring myself to tell them. I still saw the authorities as the enemy. David had made sure of that. He'd brainwashed me over the years. I believed his words of warning were true, that I had to keep my mouth shut if I was to have any chance of keeping my daughters, which seemed like the most important thing in the world. I was terrified of the man. And I didn't think for one minute that anything would come of his arrest. I was convinced that he would talk his way out of it, that he would regain control, even of the police...

'And I was *dreading* his reaction when he was freed. Because I was sure he would be. The police searched, but they didn't find the cellar. They didn't find you. The entrance was well hidden behind that dresser. Not even the dog found it. I think our house was the only one on the street with a cellar. There was nothing to suggest it was there. David seemed to be winning, which didn't surprise me in the slightest. I thought he was all-powerful, almost godlike, although calling him a devil would be a far better description. I can't begin to explain what it was like living with that man. He was poison. He polluted everything he touched. It was as if he dictated my thoughts.'

* * *

There was so much more I needed to know. So much I needed to understand. 'Do you think there was *anything* the police or social services could have said which would have made you talk? Anything at all?'

Cynthia looked up now, slowly shaking her head, eyes haunted by the past, her head craned towards me. 'They tried. Believe me, they tried. But I didn't believe a word they said. A female social worker turned up at the house a short time after David's arrest. Pam obviously knew her, they were friendly, chatty, seemingly so unthreatening, but I didn't see them that way. I still thought I had to watch what I said. Not a word out of place. Not a single word.

'I was so very wary when the social worker introduced herself to my girls and me. The woman seemed nice enough, as Pam did, but I found them terrifying. A part of me wanted to talk to them, to reach out, to try to explain the reality of my life. But both women were behaving just as David warned me that they would, with their ready smiles and kind words. I saw it as manipulation, a mechanism to trick and control me, no more than that.

'Oh, the irony! It's not lost on me. I do realise I had it completely the wrong way around. David influenced everything I did, everything I thought. Even when he wasn't there, he was inside my head. A part of me still thinks he is sometimes. I still hear his criticisms, the snide remarks. Though that doesn't often happen these days.'

I was keen to get Cynthia focusing back on the past. I was glad she was in a better place now, but she still had a story to tell. 'Okay, so Galbraith was taken away in the police car; the police officer and social worker were at the house. I was still in the cellar. Did you have any real understanding of what was going on?'

'Well, yes and no, they told me what was happening. They were careful to explain. But I still saw everything through the prism of David's lies. Elizabeth, Sarah and I were taken to a social services children's resource centre where I was told my girls would be interviewed on video and that anything they said could be potentially used in evidence. I hated the thought of them going through that. But I was confident they wouldn't say anything that could potentially incriminate David. Even then I was more scared of him than anything else. He'd done an effective job of silencing them too. I just hoped and prayed I'd get the girls back. That the social workers didn't decide they were unsafe in my care. I was a bad mother, after all. He'd said it so many times I believed it.'

'Right, so the girls were taken to be interviewed, I'm clear on that,' I said. 'But what happened to you? Were any further efforts made to encourage you to talk?'

'Oh yes, they certainly hadn't given up, not yet. A detective named Myra Thomas took me into a room, made me tea and began asking me questions. I couldn't believe someone was making *me* tea. David would never have done that, not in a million years. That one small act of kindness had me in tears. But I still thought she was pretending to be nice. That it was all a devious plan to trick me into saying something I shouldn't say.

'All I could think was that I might slip up or that the girls might have said I was a bad mother as their father so often had. The officer asked me what was upsetting me as I wiped away my tears. She told me to relax. But how could I relax? I thought I was in danger of losing my lovely girls forever. I'd never felt less relaxed in my life. Myra handed me a tissue, saying I'd had a difficult day, that my strained emotions were understandable in the circumstances. She was so very kind, so patient, but all I heard was threats. And then she started talking about my parents. I was told they'd taken my girls to their Tenby home after their video interviews. There wasn't a need for medicals. It was either my parents or foster care. Those were the choices. Having the girls home with me wasn't an option. Not until the authorities had fully assessed any risk the girls faced. And the officer couldn't even tell me how long the assessment would take. It seemed all of David's terrible warnings were coming true.'

'How did you feel about your daughters being in your parents' care?'

'I wasn't happy. They were good people, caring people, but they thought I was a bad mother too. They believed I was mentally ill, racked with uncontrollable anxiety that meant I couldn't provide consistent parental care. David had made sure of that. He talked to them often, filling their heads with lies. He'd even told them that I'd refused to allow them to visit. I hadn't seen my parents since leaving Cardiff. The officer seemed surprised when I told her that. David had alienated me from everyone by then; he became my world, my prison.'

I wondered how I would have reacted had I been the officer talking to Cynthia, looking for her cooperation, seeking evidence against a psychopathic paedophile she wasn't willing to provide. Cynthia seemed so reasonable all these years on, but back then, she must have appeared obstructive. No wonder the authorities were concerned for her daughters' safety. I don't think I'd have had the insight to see the reality. I wondered if others did.

'What was the officer's response?'

'She asked if I was scared of David.'

'And what did you say?'

'I told her that was something he wouldn't want me to talk about.'

'That must have rung alarm bells in her head.'

'Yes, I think it did. She tried to be reassuring. She told me David was in custody, locked up in a cell, that I was safe to talk, that he couldn't hurt me any more. She almost got me to open up. It was close, but sadly not close enough. I could still hear David's voice, almost as if he was there in the room, telling me not to say anything. I bit down on my tongue hard to stop myself from talking. It was the only way I could shut myself up. And then she said something that left me *really* shaken.'

'What was that?'

'She said the police needed my help, that a child was missing, a seven-year-old little boy called Anthony with short red hair and freckles. She told me what had happened to your mother and that the police suspected David of being both the attacker and abductor. She said you were in terrible danger and asked me outright if I'd seen you and if I could help them find you.

'And I said no. Can you believe that? I said *no!* It was too much to handle, too much to contemplate. She kept asking, again and again, almost pleading, increasing the pressure. But I still didn't say anything. I closed my eyes and bit down on my tongue again, tasting blood. I so wanted to tell her the truth, but I feared David's reaction if I did the wrong thing again. I told myself that if he had you, it must be for a good reason, that the consequences of my speaking out could be dire. And so, I kept my mouth shut. That seems insane to me now. I can't believe I was so foolish. But it's how it was. I wish I could tell you something different. But that's what happened. DC Thomas persevered for another twenty minutes or more, asking the same questions without getting answers.

'And then after all that, it was over, which was a huge relief. I really thought I'd done the right thing in keeping my mouth shut. I was that confused. David's influence was all-consuming. She took me home. The police had finished searching by then. They didn't find anything. David was careful, meticulous, and he hid things extremely well. She asked me all the same questions again on the journey back to the house, but I still didn't say anything. And I didn't look in the cellar either. It was out of bounds, David's territory, not my business, nothing to do with me. I behaved as if it wasn't there. I hate to admit that to you of all people, but it's true. I'm so very sorry about that now. I hope you can accept my apologies.'

* * *

Cynthia had given me a lot of her time. She'd engaged in the interview process with openness and extraordinary honesty, sometimes at an obvious emotional cost to herself. I wanted to be understanding. I tried to be patient and not to let my agitation show. But it wasn't easy. I'd experienced Galbraith's manipulation up close and personal. I knew the extent to which he went to control. But Cynthia's story still surprised and angered me. I'm not immune to emotion. The woman knew I was in that cellar, and yet she said nothing. Worse still, she did nothing. I still find that hard to accept. I ordered a bottle of Dutch lager, something to take the edge off as she continued her story. I sat there closed-mouthed and let her talk.

'I can remember how good it felt to be home alone without David in the house. I fantasised about a future without him – just my girls and me, happy and carefree when they returned from their grandparents' care. But I feared it was a desperate female fantasy and no more than that. Good things didn't happen in my life, and they hadn't for a very long time. I believed David would soon be back, angry and menacing, that he'd outsmart the police and win in the end. And as unlikely as it seems, it turned out my fears were correct. My world was about to become an even darker place. David did outwit them. It wouldn't be long until he was home. They let the bastard out on bail.'

'How the hell did that happen?'

'God knows. David had a lot of contacts, he networked, maybe it was that.'

'So, he came back to the house?'

'Yes, yes, he did.'

'That must have been frightening for you.' I guess I was stating the obvious, but she replied anyway.

'It was terrifying, totally terrifying, but not surprising in many ways. I always thought David would win.'

'So, what happened that day, the day he was released?'

'Do you want to hear it all?'

'Yeah, I do, right from the start.'

She blew the air slowly from her mouth as her chest rose and fell. 'That's one day of my life I'm never going to forget. I only wish I could. My alarm clock woke me, I got up early as usual while it was still dark, and I rushed downstairs on autopilot to start making breakfast to David's precise requirements. And then it suddenly dawned on me. I was alone in the house. He wouldn't be coming down the stairs. There would be no criticisms, complaints or threats, not that morning. I wouldn't be prodded, pushed, punched or kicked for making some mistake or other that he was only too ready to pounce on. There was only me in that big old house. But I knew he'd be back. I'd never been more sure of anything in my life. So, I couldn't let my standards slip. If I did, there'd be a price to pay, bruising, maybe even cuts, not where it showed, never where it showed. Everything had to be perfect for his eventual return. So, I got on with the housework, hoovering, polishing, dusting, all the time trying to forget that my girls were not with me.

'I was getting more and more anxious as the minutes ticked by, expecting to hear a key in the door, his footsteps on the hall tiles, his angry roar when he first saw me, the first blow of his hand. I watched and listened and waited in frightened anticipation, dreading his inevitable appearance and whatever suffering that would bring.

'And then the phone rang shortly before twelve. I rushed to the hall and picked it up, hoping it was news of my girls and dreading it was David. But it wasn't either of those things. I recognised Detective Inspector Gravel's voice as soon as I heard it. I opened my mouth as if to speak, but I couldn't find the words. They stuck in my throat. I listened in silence as he told me that David had been charged with some grave offences but that he'd been granted bail by the magistrates pending Crown Court trial, that he'd be coming home. Gravel seemed more shocked than I was. I could hear it in his tone.

'I found my voice then. Not to ask what the charges were, but if David knew the detective was calling. Can you believe that? That's what concerned me the most. That David would know I'd talked to the inspector without his permission. But then DI Gravel said things I wasn't expecting, things which somehow made me question my reaction to his call.'

I sat upright in my seat, gulping my lager, emptying most of the bottle, keen to know more. How had Gravel succeeded when others had failed? 'What did he say to you?'

'He told me to get out of there. That David was a very dangerous man. That he'd committed some truly awful offences against children, that I didn't have much time, that I should escape while I still had the chance. He was a good detective, an officer who cared. A man who was prepared to do the right thing.'

'And did you escape?'

'I can't explain why his words had such a sudden impact after all that time. But they were a wake-up call. They hit me hard. It was as if he'd switched a light on in my head. He'd spoken with such urgency, such conviction. I knew then that I had to face reality, however difficult, however traumatic. And I knew that you were a victim of my husband's violence. There was no more room for denial. The truth was staring me in the face. I had to act, for you, for me, and my girls.

'Looking back, I know I should have said something to DI Gravel. I should have told him about the cellar. But I didn't. I wasn't thinking straight. I sat in the kitchen and stared at the dresser, trying to build up enough courage to push it aside. I needed to see the evidence for myself. I needed to see you were really there. Maybe then I'd have the courage to dial 999.

'Even then, a part of me was still in denial. I can remember my entire body trembling when I finally pushed the dresser aside. It took all my effort, all my strength. And then the steps; I thought my legs might give way at any moment as I forced myself down the grey concrete staircase towards a steel door at the bottom. I so wanted to retreat and run, but I urged myself on, one footstep at a time. If you were there, I had to see. I had to help. I'd sat on the sidelines for far too long. I lost control of my bladder as I pushed open the security door, peering into the darkness. I stood there staring, allowing my eyesight to adapt to the gloom, dreading what I might find. I called out, but there was no reply, just a silence that seemed to mock me. I searched for a light, groping for a switch until I finally found one on the wall inside the cellar to the left of the door.'

She stalled, clearing her throat before speaking again.

'It took some courage to flick that switch. In those circumstances, darkness was my friend. But I knew I had to do it, and quickly, too, before David's return. I had to shelter my eyes from the bright electric glare as I stepped into the white-tiled cellar for the first time. At first, I didn't see you, hanging naked, shackled to that wall with a clear plastic tube down your throat. I didn't see the video equipment or the black leather hoods, or the instruments of torture. All I saw was a clinical white room that was strangely reassuring, reminding me as it did of an operating theatre or other medical facilities. That's what I told myself as I searched for solace, desperate to deny the awful reality.'

I said nothing, listening horrified as Cynthia continued her story.

'I turned in a slow circle, scanning the room, and there was no more room for denial. I wept as I looked at you, pale and emaciated. I touched your face and knew you were real. My husband was a monster. Why hadn't I seen it before? I thought for a terrible moment that you were dead. That I'd acted too late. I don't think I'd ever have forgiven myself were that the case.'

Cynthia took a shallow breath and continued.

'But there was a warmth to your skin. I found a faint heartbeat. I tried desperately to free you from the metal shackles until my nails were broken and my fingers bled. But it was hopeless. I searched frantically for a key but with no success. I was never going to get you off that wall, however hard I tried. I had to summon help. I had to get to the phone before David returned. It seemed your only chance and mine too.

'I'd now seen what he was capable of. I knew his secrets. It was a case of escape or die. I ran for the steps, leaping two at a time, panting hard as I stumbled into the kitchen. But then I stopped, my worst fears a reality, as I heard the unmistakable sound of the front door opening and then being slammed shut. He was back; the bastard was back. I was too slow. I'd never felt such terror. But there was a new determination too. I pictured you hanging on that wall in my husband's version of hell, and I knew I was willing to do everything I could to save your life. If I was going down, I was going down fighting.'

There were tears running down Cynthia's face as it all came back to her.

'And then he appeared at the kitchen door, yelling, striding towards me, upping the tension, burning with rage. I'd seen him angry many times, but never that angry. He was like a wild beast, snarling, baring his teeth. I forced myself to change positions, moving away from him, searching for a weapon, any weapon, with quick darting eyes. He laughed as I reached for a knife, gripping the shaft tightly in my right hand, fearful of dropping it, almost too scared to hold it out in front of me. I stood between David and the steps, telling myself to be brave, not to crumble, to stay strong despite what seemed impossible odds. And then we fought, something I thought I'd never do, a life and death struggle. David punching and kicking, and me thrusting ineffectually with the blade. He hit me once, then again, bang, knocking me to the floor. I finally landed a significant strike to his upper thigh when lying prone and close to passing out. He was losing a good deal of blood as he stepped over me, stamping down, heading for the steps. Even in my disoriented, barely conscious state I felt certain he intended to kill you and to kill me too. I blinked my eyes repeatedly as I gradually came round. It only took seconds, thank God, any longer, it would have been too late.

'I'd never felt such pain or fear. Blood was pouring from a fractured nose, my ribs were broken, I was struggling to breathe, but I wasn't ready to give up the fight. If it had only been me, I'd very likely have given up. I might even have welcomed death. But I needed to live for my girls and for you too. There was no other choice. I crawled across the kitchen floor, reaching the cellar entrance and pulling myself to my feet with the aid of an overturned chair as David was reaching the bottom step. I was running out of time. Your life was hanging by a thread. I stumbled down the steps, finally entering the cellar to find David preparing a syringe and needle. He laughed and then told me he was going to execute you, and then me, ensuring I'd suffer terribly in the process. I think he thought he was indestructible.

That he could get away with anything. That he could murder with impunity. But he was wrong. Justice came from the last place he'd expected.'

'What did you do?'

Cynthia smiled, the expression lighting up her face as the years melted away, a girlish glint in her eye I hadn't seen before. 'I killed him. He was distracted by the idea of administering the lethal injection. He was about to plunge the needle deep into your gut. I don't think he saw me as a threat, not in my state. It gave me the opportunity I needed. I wanted him dead, and I made sure it happened. Simply overpowering him wasn't enough. I needed the threat he posed gone forever. I stabbed and kept stabbing. I couldn't stop once I'd started, even after he was inca-pacitated. I slashed, and I stabbed, and I'd never felt more alive. Years of pent-up rage poured out of me. I could see he was still breathing when he fell to the floor. So, I stabbed him some more, time and again, until I completely obliterated his features.

'Now it really was over. And it felt so good. The vicious bastard was no longer a threat to me or anybody else. I rested there next to David's corpse for a few minutes, regaining my strength. There was blood and gore everywhere. I was covered in the stuff. That's not an easy thing to admit. The fact that I lay there now seems bizarre, even to me. But I was close to exhaus-tion. Adrenaline had kept me going. I was too tired to move. And David was dead. That was a huge relief. The tension melted away. I was alive, you were alive, my girls were safe, and my world was a better place. I didn't think about the possible repercussions at that stage. That came later. I was just glad to be free of him. A dark cloud had lifted, letting in the light.'

I drained the dregs of my beer, ordering another bottle as the impact of Cynthia's story truly hit me. I'd been so very close to death. Within seconds of breathing my last. 'My parents haven't told me any of this. Thank you so much for saving my life. You showed enormous courage.'

Cynthia smiled again, acknowledging my words of gratitude and admiration with a single nod of her head. 'I dialled 999 a short time later once I gained sufficient strength to return to the hallway. I remember sitting on the lounge carpet listening to music after making the call, Bowie, a favourite LP I hadn't dared play for years. David frowned on modern music. He didn't listen to anything but classical. And that meant I didn't either. It was always his choice, never mine. Now I could listen to what I wanted to.

'He'd have hated that. It was a seminal moment, a joy. It was another victory of sorts. I was dancing to the music despite my injuries when I first heard the sound of sirens. And then an ambulance, the police and the fire service all arrived within minutes of each other. I saw two firefighters carrying some kind of cutting equipment into the house as I was driven off in the back of a police car. That helped my mood. I knew you'd get the help you needed. And the arresting officers seemed friendly enough, supportive. I wasn't handcuffed. They appeared to understand why I'd done what I did.

'But they had a job to do. I'd killed a man. It was only as we approached the police station that the possibility of a prison sentence finally crossed my mind. That didn't worry me a great deal, not on a personal level. I guess it was the obvious conclusion to events. And anywhere would be better than living with David, even prison. But the idea of being without my lovely girls was hard to bear. That did concern me. I think it was the only thing that did.'

* * *

I pondered Cynthia's statement as she paused, sipping her tea. A potential prison sentence seemed harsh in the circumstances. Cynthia deserved a medal for bravery. I'd happily pin it on her chest loud and proud. But in the eyes of British law, it was murder. Incarceration seemed an inevitable end to her tale. Where's the justice in that? I asked her if she'd served a sentence. I knew the answer was yes, having read it in an old newspaper article at the local library, but I wanted to hear if from her, in her words. I felt she had a right to tell her own story. And journalists don't always get all the facts right.

'Were you sent to prison?'

'Yes, yes, I was, I was sentenced to sixteen years. There was a campaign to free me, women's groups and my mother did what they could. But my lawyer needed new evidence – something on which to base an appeal. I taught English to some of the other women. And Mum brought my girls to visit me when she could. It was never easy seeing them in that place, but I was always pleased they'd come. I'd given up on being released by that time. I was adapting to my new life because I had to. But then, after three long years, something wonderful happened. My lawyer came to the prison. DI Gravel had been in touch with my legal team. The new owners of David's house had pulled up the floorboards to fit a new central heating system. They found a huge collection of files, photographs and videos hidden under a false floor. One of those files was dedicated to *me*. And the contents proved that *everything* I'd said was true.

'David had kept a detailed written record of everything he'd done to me from day one. It was a complete game-changer. Everything I was subjected to meant diminished responsibility. I was suffering an abnormality of the mind at the time of the killing. I think that's the legal wording. My lawyer began the appeals process straight away. I was finally released about nine months later when the court substituted my murder conviction with the lesser charge of manslaughter. And best of all, the judges decided I'd already served enough time in prison. Four years after I was first convicted, I was a free woman. It was an incredible moment when I walked free for the first time. I wrote a book about it. My mother, of all people, convinced me it was a tale worth telling.'

'A book, really? I haven't come across it,' I said.

'I wrote a fictionalised account based on the facts. It was published under a different name, a pseudonym, not my own. I didn't want the attention, not after everything that was said in the papers.'

'Is it still available?'

'Um, maybe, I think so, although it's been a while since I looked. It may be out of print. I haven't had any royalties for ages.'

'Why didn't you say something before?'

'The time never seemed right. And I didn't sell many copies. I wrote it as a cautionary story more than anything else. Some people found it interesting. There were a few decent reviews. I can give you a copy, if you like? I've still got one somewhere.'

'Yeah, please, that would be appreciated.'

I committed to reading Cynthia's book when she gave me the copy. There would be some parallels with mine; that's inevitable. But many of our experiences were very different too.

* * *

I asked her how her life had gone when she was finally released. This seemed one part of her story she was happy to share. She took obvious pleasure in the telling.

'I moved back to live with Mum, Dad and my two wonderful girls in Tenby. It was a case of starting over, moving ahead, slowly regaining my confidence and not letting the past drag me down.

There were dark times, but in the main, I was coping. And my parents were nothing but helpful, providing support as I needed it. They so regretted being taken in by David's lies. But they made up for it once they knew the truth.'

'That's good to hear.'

'I got a part-time job in a local restaurant at the start of that first summer back in Tenby and made good use of my free time. We were lucky to be living in such a beautiful part of the world. I took my girls to the beach. We did a lot of swimming. My dad even bought a small sailing boat for us all to use. I still suffered nightmares; I still felt on edge a lot of the time, and trusting others was difficult. But I don't want to over-stress the negatives. Everything was going pretty well, all considered. My memories of the bad times faded as time passed. I even got in touch with your mother.'

'Really?'

'Hasn't she told you?'

I shook my head. 'No, she hasn't, not a word.'

'She'd visited me once in prison, thanking me for saving your life. And then we met a couple of times after my release to share pleasantries over a drink or a coffee. She told me of your recovery. How well you were doing. But I never saw you again as a child. It's as if things have gone full circle. I'm glad we've met again now.'

I told Cynthia that I was glad too. And I meant it. Meeting her again was a pleasure. Although, of course, I couldn't remember the first time given my unconscious state. I'll always be grateful for that.

I hugged Cynthia before leaving the café that day. I felt an affection for her, a warmth I hadn't expected. She'd gone from villain to hero in my eyes, admired for her courage and resilience. It's a reality that our preconceptions can be all too inaccurate as we seek to make our world a more straightforward place.

I'd expected Cynthia's story to be so very different from the reality. I'm not saying she's perfect. Who is? She's so very far from that. And I'm sure she could say the same of me. But she was a victim of circumstances, as I was. She drew the short straw, as I did. I feel obliged to accept that.

As for the rest, I'll give her the benefit of the doubt. We have a bond, an affinity born of adversity. I hope we stay in touch. I hope she considers me a friend. I owe her. And she's a survivor, too.

28

My mother had told me of my admission to South Wales General Hospital following my rescue from Galbraith's cellar hell.

She was in one ward, slowly recovering from her severe beating, and I was in another, still unconscious at first, but soon back in the land of the living thanks to expert medical care.

Mother told me she was far more relieved by my gradual recovery than by her own. She insisted on being taken by wheelchair to my bedside each day until I was ready to be discharged home to my father's care. My mother and father were back together by then. It was hardly a marriage made in heaven, it never was, and it never will be. They'd be the first to admit that. But they were doing their best to rescue their relationship after my father's infidelity. I think, for the most part, they put it behind them.

It's only now that I'm a parent myself that I realise how brutal my abduction must have been for them both. They'd been through a nightmare and came out the other side. Not unscathed, that would be too much to ask. But we were a family again despite Galbraith's best efforts, all four of us together in our cottage home.

I remembered nothing of my time in that terrible place, the netherworld Galbraith created in an ordinary house in a typical Georgian suburban street. One Friday night, I went to bed at home, and I woke up in a children's hospital ward days later. The time in between didn't register. And no one spoke of what had happened, not a hint, not a word, nothing to fill in the gaps. Obviously, I knew that something had gone very wrong. That would have been blatantly obvious to a person of any age, child or not. I'd quickly lost some weight and strength, my arms and shoulders were painful, and my throat was raw red, making swallowing difficult. And I could witness my mother's injuries when she visited me on the children's ward. They were impossible to miss. Her face was something akin to a Halloween mask, swollen, cut and bruised. But the cause remained a mystery.

Nobody told me what had happened, and for some reason, I didn't ask. I think something told me my questions wouldn't be welcome. And I didn't want to do or say anything to rock the boat. Only weeks later, when a Welsh television news reporter talked of Galbraith's death and his wife's imprisonment, did I begin to put two and two together. A seven-year-old boy had been rescued from a cellar below Galbraith's home, an unconscious boy, a boy who was now recovering in the care of his parents. The boy wasn't named or even described beyond this, but I strongly suspected he was me. I recalled my visit to Galbraith's clinic, the film, that awful film, his threats, the way he'd scared me, and watching that news report, it all seemed clear. I'd been abducted, I'd been imprisoned. It had all merged in my head, the horror of it all. It was imprinted on my mind.

The facts fitted. It all made sense and answered my unasked questions. I came up with a hypothesis and was sure I was correct. As it happens, in the main I was. But it was years later when my mother confirmed my suspicions and only then because I gave her no choice.

If I hadn't seen that news report, who knows? Maybe my life wouldn't have been so dominated by thoughts of that time. Maybe Galbraith wouldn't have played such a big part in my life. Perhaps my many flashbacks and nightmares were more to do with what I'd learned than actual memories, or it could have been a combination of both. That's something I can never answer with any certainty. I think perhaps the way my parents chose to deal with our family trauma was misguided. I believe an honest age-appropriate discussion would have been best, combined with whatever reassurance was needed. But they did their best under challenging circumstances. That's all anyone can do. I'll put that on record. I'm grateful to them for that.

29

I've decided to call it soul-searching, my looking back on the writing process, weighing up the pros and cons, although self-obsession may be a more accurate way of putting it. I planned on an evaluation when I reached this stage of the book. I was intending to explore what went well or not so well. Whether or not the process had been a valuable therapeutic exercise, as cathartic as I'd hoped.

I thought I'd simply be talking about my state of mind, my relationships, whether I'd found a degree of peace previously out of my reach, and if my reliance on the mind-numbing effects of alcohol had been mitigated either wholly or at least in part. But things didn't work out that way, not even close. Sometimes our actions, however well-intentioned, can lead to unforeseen consequences. And that has certainly been the case for me.

Events took a dramatic turn as my book approached its end. There's no easy way of saying this, no way of softening the blow. This final chapter was written in a cell, a small space, bars on the windows, bunk beds, and a locked steel door. I'm back at Swansea Prison. Not as a visitor this time, but on remand for murder.

Not exactly the outcome I envisaged when I began writing my story, but life sometimes takes an unexpected turn. I'm not going to plead my innocence as many do here, because the evidence against me is impossible to deny. I killed Gary Davies, and for a good reason too.

I did it, I'm guilty, I confess, and I feel no remorse. My only regret is the inevitably negative impact my actions will have on my family. For that, I am genuinely sorry. But all I can do is offer mitigation, both to them and to you.

I very much hope everyone sympathises and understands at least to a degree when they know the full facts. Circumstances dictated my actions. That's the truth of it, it was as simple as that.

Gary Davies was a hard man to forget. I thought of him often after receiving that letter. I thought of the damage he'd done, the conspiratorial role he'd played in my abduction, and the threat he'd pose when released. He was poison. He offered nothing but misery.

And then I saw him, released, a free man, on the street, watching as I collected Olivia from school one rainy wet winter afternoon. Davies was standing there dressed in a knee-length navy-blue raincoat with the hood up, looking with interest at each young child in turn as they left the school building with a parent or guardian, blissfully oblivious to the predatory beast standing only yards away.

He grinned, waving when he recognised me, and then he focused on Olivia, walking towards us with a lascivious leer on his otherwise unremarkable face. Can you imagine the bare-faced cheek of the man, the brazen threat he posed? I felt my anger rise inside me as he commented on Olivia's appearance, saying how nice she looked, how innocent, how pretty. And I knew then that I had to do something to alleviate the risk the predator posed. The authorities were clearly failing in that responsibility, so I knew it was down to me.

The sense of parental responsibility was overwhelming. I felt a strong desire to attack, to pummel Davies to a bloody pulp right there and then until he was no longer a danger to my child or any other. But I held myself back. I didn't want to resort to violence unless it was unavoidable. Yet I knew I had to do something. The public notifications I'd previously considered now seemed wholly inadequate in the light of events.

So, I planned to see Davies alone, to warn him off, to scare the life out of him, to keep him away. And I did only intend to scare him. I want to make that clear. If I had to assault him to achieve my desired outcome, I was willing to do it. But only if there was no other choice. A last resort, but no more than that.

Nicola collected Olivia from school the next day and the day after that. But I was there, too, watching from a distance, parked in a rented car. Davies made another appearance on the second day, hidden behind a convenient red-brick wall this time, taking photographs with a smartphone when a particular child caught his interest. I watched him, but he didn't see me. I followed when he rode off on an old red and white moped about ten minutes later. It was only a short drive to where the predator lived, a bedsit on the ground floor of a three-storey building in a busy street lined with shops, cafés and restaurants.

He entered the building, a light shone bright, he appeared at a window before drawing the curtains, and I knew exactly where to find him. I took a six-inch hunting knife from the glove box of my rental car, walked towards his front door, one step, two steps, encouraging myself on, thinking back to my childhood, the confusion, the fear, the sadness. I never intended to kill Davies; that's the truth of it. I was there to scare him, to *terrify* him, but no more than that. To tell him never to *dare* come anywhere near my daughter on pain of death. But it didn't work out that way. I pressed the lowest of three doorbells, only waiting a short time until Davies opened the door. I told him why I was there, holding the knife in plain sight, ordering him to stay away, threatening violence if he didn't comply.

But then he laughed. He asked where my pretty little girl was, licking his lips slowly, first the top and then the bottom, poking his tongue out again and again. It was too much to take as a red mist descended. I remember the shock on the predator's face when I pushed him back into the hallway and drew back the knife with a snarl. He stared at me, frozen in indecision, unable to move as I plunged the point of the blade deep into his gut, hitting bone, almost jarring the weapon from my hand. A gasp became a groan as he sank slowly to the floor, begging for help, desperate to hang onto his worthless life as I stood back, watching him die. I felt a surge of panic as he drew his last breath, but there was a sense of satisfaction too. He'd threatened my daughter, my little girl, and that threat was real. Davies had damaged so many innocent lives, but Olivia's wouldn't be another. When I think of that now, I'm glad the bastard's dead. I have to admit, I wish he'd suffered more.

I saw one of the town's recently installed security cameras fixed high on a building immediately opposite as I walked away from the bedsit. And in that instant, I suspected my fate was sealed. I returned home, where I drank whisky from the bottle, thoroughly cleaned the knife, washed my clothes, and tried to act as if nothing out of the ordinary had happened when Nicola and Olivia returned from town. A part of me still hoped I'd get away with the killing, that the camera wasn't working, that no one else had seen.

But deep down, I knew that not to be true. There was a lens focused on me as I committed my execution and likely witnesses too. I wasn't alone in the street that day as I hurried back towards my car with the knife in my bloody hand.

I waited for the sound of sirens, the rat-tat-tat of the police knocking on my door. And soon, my fearful anticipation became a sad reality. I was arrested about twenty minutes later, dragged from the house in handcuffs as my wife and child looked on, incredulous, asking questions I chose not to answer.

* * *

I'm now reluctantly resigned to a life behind bars as I await my trial and sentence. My mother, father, sister and wife have all visited me twice in the three weeks I've been here, and all plan to come again. I'm grateful for that. Truly I am. But I hope they can get on with their lives and put the past behind them as I so failed to do. I hope they're not haunted by events as I was.

Galbraith shaped my life in so many ways. I was unable to let him go. I don't want my actions to ruin my family's lives as the wicked doctor did mine. Nicola didn't bring Olivia when she made the journey. She doesn't think this is a place for children. That upset me at first, and it hit me in the gut like a physical blow. But given time to think, I've concluded Nicola may well be correct. And Olivia is young enough to forget. Maybe she should put me behind her too. She'll likely be an adult by the time I get out of here.

I plan to plead guilty when my court date finally arrives. So, I won't be free anytime soon.

This is my confession, the truth and nothing but the truth, my story told in my own words.

ACKNOWLEDGMENTS

With thanks to my editor, Tara Loder, and to the rest of the brilliant Boldwood Books team.

MORE FROM JOHN NICHOLL

We hope you enjoyed reading *The Father*. If you did, please leave a review.

If you'd like to gift a copy, this book is also available as a paperback, digital audio download and audiobook CD.

The Sisters, another gripping psychological thriller by John Nicholl, is available to order now.

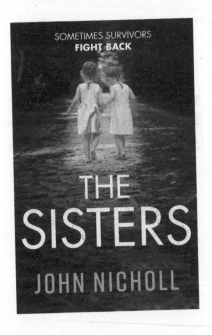

ABOUT THE AUTHOR

John Nicholl is an award-winning, bestselling author of numerous darkly psychological suspense thrillers, previously published by Bloodhound. These books have a gritty realism born of his real-life experience as an ex-police officer and child protection social worker.

Visit John's website: https://www.johnnicholl.com

Follow John on social media:

 twitter.com/nicholl06

 facebook.com/JohnNichollAuthor

 instagram.com/johnnichollauthor

Boldwood

Boldwood Books is an award-winning fiction publishing company seeking out the best stories from around the world.

Find out more at www.boldwoodbooks.com

Join our reader community for brilliant books, competitions and offers!

Follow us
@BoldwoodBooks
@BookandTonic

Sign up to our weekly deals newsletter

https://bit.ly/BoldwoodBNewsletter